SICK
pleasure

JESSICA
SERRA HUIZENGA

books by

JESSICA SERRA HUIZENGA

Crazy Beautiful Series
Crazy Beautiful (Book 1)
Mad Addiction (Book 2)
Sick Pleasure (Book 3)

Author's Note
While each story in the Crazy Beautiful Series can be read as a standalone book, I recommend reading them in order to fully understand the world and characters.

Hazel Blake loves Tristan Sharp.
Tristan Sharp hates Hazel Blake.

There is only one word to describe Hazel Blake and Tristan Sharp: *history*. Intense, painful, passionate history. (OK, four words.)

But it's been over five years now and Hazel's ready to leave the past behind. Having nobody but an absent father, a crazy mother, and a preoccupied brother means she could really use her old friend again. So what if she still has deeper feelings for Tristan? She knows she majorly screwed things up and doesn't deserve him anymore, so she'll settle for anything he might be willing to give—even if it's just his body.

When Hazel comes storming back into Tristan's life, opening all sorts of old wounds, he wants nothing more than to get to the forgetting part. But he's also having trouble with the whole forgiveness thing, too. When the girl you love rips your heart out and tosses it around like a beanbag, it tends to change a guy. But nobody gets under Tristan's skin like Hazel, so he just needs to get her out of his system, right? Hit it and quit it. For good this time, and nobody ever needs to know.

Yes, everything that went down between Hazel and Tristan is in the past.

Too bad history is about to repeat itself . . .

What happens when you love the person you hate?
Can people that hurt each other heal together?

"I will bruise your lips and scar your
knees and love you too hard.
I will destroy you in the most beautiful way possible
And when I leave you will finally
understand why storms are named after people.

ROCK BOTTOM

CHAPTER

one

Tristan

"WOW. THAT WAS . . . you are . . . *wow*."

"Tell me something I don't know." I glance at the naked, satisfied blonde lying next to me in my bed, trying to remember her name. Jenny? Julia? Definitely something that starts with a J . . .

I lean back against the pillows and let my breathing return to normal. In my opinion the sex was nothing to write home about, but despite this chick's annoying high-pitched screeches and over-exaggerated porn star moans, I have to give her props for stamina. At one point I was pounding into her so hard from behind that I thought I might split her in two, but she took it like a champ and only moaned louder each time I bottomed out.

Now I'm sure her pussy sees more action than Schwarzenegger—as evidenced by the wide assortment of condoms she whipped out of her purse earlier—but you've got to give a girl points for enthusiasm.

After a few seconds I open my eyes and look at the clock on my bedside table. Ten thirteen p.m. I have to be up in six hours to get an early start on the Jeffrie's house addition over on Maple

Street. Sleep might be a good idea.

I push myself off the bed. The floor is littered with various articles of clothing that were ripped off as we stumbled into the room: a work boot here, a hot-pink stiletto there. I wade through the mess of dark jeans and cheap lace and grab a pair of shorts from the bottom drawer of my dresser. I pull them on and head for the kitchen to get a drink, leaving what's-her-name still panting on the bed. Some girls get dressed right after we're finished while others like to hang around. It really doesn't matter to me either way. If she leaves I can get some shut-eye in peace, and if she doesn't, well, then there's always the possibility of an encore.

I finish more than half a water bottle in one swig and, as I'm wiping my mouth on the back of my hand, the girl comes sauntering out of the bedroom. Still naked.

She reaches around me to help herself to what's in the fridge and makes a disappointed sound in the back of her throat before grabbing a bottle of Yuengling.

"Typical guy, nothing but beer," she mutters while poking around the kitchen for a bottle opener.

I reach beside her into a drawer and pull one out, taking the beer from her hand to pop the top off. I hand it back. "There's water, too."

She takes a sip from the bottle, ignoring my comment. "Your whole apartment looks empty. Did you just move in or something?"

I shake my head and look around the one-bedroom apartment that I've lived in for five years. Off the narrow galley kitchen is a small living room with a simple brown couch, wooden coffee table, and a flat-screen TV mounted on the wall. To the right is the bedroom with all the essentials—you know: bed, dresser, bedside table. Across from my room is the bathroom—toilet, shower, sink. Sure, it's not much, but what more does a twenty-eight-year-old, unattached guy need?

"I like to keep things simple," I answer.

She shrugs, not all that interested, and takes another drink before putting her bottle on the counter. She moves in front of me, pushing her tits against my bare chest, and playfully bites my bottom lip. I can taste the beer on her breath.

"Let me go pee and then we can have sex again." She runs her fingers down my chest and disappears around the corner into the bathroom.

I guess she plans to stay a while. I can sleep when I'm dead, right?

I finish the rest of my water and head back to the bedroom. My cell phone rings and I grab it from the nightstand. When I see the name that flashes across the screen, my stomach drops.

Hazel Blake.

Why the fuck is she calling me?

Hazel and I have known each other since we were kids, but we haven't talked much in the past five years—not since she ripped my heart out of my chest with her bare hands and tossed it aside like it was nothing but a piece of shitty garbage. That kind of thing tends to fuck up a relationship.

I'm still tight with her brother, Ryan, though, so she and I occasionally still see each other during a family party or something. But since nobody knows what went down between us, we'll usually just exchange civil pleasantries and keep it moving. It's been years since she's called me directly.

And OK, 'tight' may be a bit of a stretch to describe my relationship with her brother. Ryan Blake *tolerates* me. Truth is, ever since some shit happened in high school, our friendship has been tense. Dude had his own issues back then and he needed someone to blame for it all. Since we still run with the same group of friends we've learned to avoid the past and can be cool as long as

I never bring up his sister, which I don't. It's not worth it to re-hash all that shit now that we're adults, so that's just the way it is. I've learned to live with it—with the past staying in the past like it fucking should—but Hazel calling me at 10:30 on a random Tuesday night is like a violent, unexpected storm that breaks the dam I've spent years building. Harsh memories start flooding back, hard and fast.

A hand snaking around my waist snaps me back to the present. "Forget the phone. Kayla wants to play again," Kayla says in an annoying baby voice as she slides her fingers south.

So much for remembering this chick's name.

The phone continues to ring. I may have nothing to say to Hazel, but if she's in trouble . . .

I grab Kayla's wrist just before she reaches her intended target. "Hold on, I need to take this."

I pick up. "Hello?"

A quiet second passes and my pulse quickens before I hear the light, husky voice that still makes my heart do weird shit inside my chest. "Tristan?"

My fingers tighten around the phone. "Hazel? Are you OK?"

"Yeah, of course."

I sink onto the bed, letting out the breath I didn't realize I was holding. She casually adds, "How are you?"

As if on cue, Kayla reaches for my junk again. Between trying to keep this girl's damn paws off of my dick and figuring out why the fuck Hazel called, I groan. Then I pretend like I'm clearing my throat and respond with a curt, "I'm good," while pulling Kayla's hand away. This elicits an over-exaggerated pouty face before she flops back on the pillows beside me.

Hazel sounds apologetic as she says, "I know it's kind of late. I'm not interrupting anything, am I?"

I glance at Kayla, who grabs her phone. "Nothing

important," I answer truthfully. I met this girl an hour ago at a bar and she practically threw herself at me, which was both desperate and sad, but hey, I'm always up for some fun.

Kayla giggles loudly at something on her screen. I'm sure Hazel hears it, but she doesn't say anything. "So what's up? I'm sure you didn't call me out of the blue just to shoot the shit, right?" I sit back against the headboard, crossing my free hand over my chest, which is still pounding like a fucking jackhammer.

Without missing a beat she responds, "Gee, I don't remember you being so charming."

From her teasing tone I know she's just trying to be playful, but for some reason hearing her dismiss our past, no matter how innocently, has me feeling defensive. I grip my phone and without thinking I bite out, "Yeah, well, there's a lot I wish *I* didn't remember."

My words hang heavily in the air before Hazel finally clears her throat, speaking softer and faster. "Listen, I was just calling since I know you're going to my brother's baby shower this weekend. Ry doesn't want our mom to know about it and I don't have a car right now so I need a ride. I would normally ask Ryan, but since it's his party he's going to be busy and I really don't want him to have to come all the way out here to get me first. Making him chauffeur his little sister to his own baby shower would be kinda messed up, right? So I figure if you're going anyway it might not be such a big deal for you to bring me, too . . ."

Her rambling is almost cute, seeing as it's a complete one-eighty from her previous easygoing attitude. The girl I remember always babbled when she was nervous. I almost let myself get caught up in thinking about the Hazel Blake I used to know, but a throat clearing on the other end of the call has me blurting out, "And I'm the only one you could think to call?" I swing my legs off the bed and silently curse myself, dropping my head in my right hand and running my fingers through my hair in frustration. I don't necessarily mean to be an asshole, but I'm trying to process the fact that I haven't heard from this girl in over five years and she's calling me to ask such a mundane favor. Like we're still friends or something.

As if reading my mind, she says, "Come on, we're still friends, right?" She chuckles. While the laugh sounds forced, there is also a genuine sad, hopeful note to her voice.

Logically I shouldn't feel the tiniest bit obligated to help the girl who broke me, but fuck, nobody's ever accused me of being smart.

"You know your brother will shit his pants to see us together." I stall, trying to get out of this. While it *is* true Ryan won't be happy, I know I can handle him. But being alone with Hazel? *Shit.*

"If he gets mad you brought me that's his problem," Hazel counters. "It's either that or I don't go at all. Unfortunately, I don't have any other options."

I sigh, out of excuses and already exhausted from our brief exchange. "I'll pick you up Saturday at two."

I hear her take a deep breath before replying, "Thanks, Tristan, really."

Hearing her sound so sincere while my name falls heavily from her lips has my head feeling fifty more shades of fucked up. To think she still has any sort of power over me causes all my douchey defenses to go up again. "I'm sure I can think of a way for you to repay me," I taunt.

But just when I think I have the upper hand, Hazel lowers her voice and says seductively, "I'm counting on it," before disconnecting the call.

Fuck. Fuck. Fuck.

CHAPTER

two

Tristan

FOUR DAYS LATER I FIND myself pulling up outside Hazel's house. Well, technically her mom's huge-ass mansion. As I punch in the code she gave me for the gate I involuntarily think about the first time I came here as a kid. With its intricately carved columns and huge windows the place practically looks like a castle, so I thought Hazel was a real-life princess or something. Goes to show you what kind of stupid crap runs through an eight-year-old's head, but I guess living in a foster home made me prefer made up stories to real life. No wonder I was such a naïve little shit. There may have been a time when I thought Hazel needed me to rescue her, but that turned out to be a bunch of bullshit. A rich, selfish girl like Hazel Blake doesn't need me for anything other than her own benefit.

If I really think about it, though, I guess Hazel did me a favor by teaching me early on that I shouldn't take anyone too seriously and that it's best to keep my emotions in check. No matter what I might be feeling on the inside, nobody else gives a shit on the outside. Most people are selfish by nature—myself included—and the sooner I understood this fact of life, the easier mine got. Life is actually pretty fucking simple: work your balls off at your job, sweat your balls off in the gym, bury yourself balls deep in the bedroom, and if anyone gives you shit, bust *their* balls. See? Easy. That heart on your sleeve? Cover that shit up. It only complicates things. Just work hard, play harder and don't give a shit what anyone else thinks.

I pull up the drive and, per her request, text Hazel to let her know I'm outside. Before she responds I give myself a little pep talk: *OK, man, this is no big deal. Keep it simple, keep it light, and just get this day over with by keeping your mouth shut . . . and your dick in your pants.*

A minute later I see Hazel coming out of the pool house, though all I can see are a slim pair of legs covered in dark jeans. Her face is blocked since she's carrying a huge box wrapped in silver paper, but I can see the colored ink of her tattoos peeking out from the sleeves of a red T-shirt. That's all it takes for my traitorous dick to twitch to life. I curse and get out of the car, jogging around the back to lower the tailgate on my pickup.

"Jesus, did you get a big enough gift?" I ask as she struggles to slide it onto the bed of the truck.

"Yeah right. This is from my grams. I've had to hide it from my mother for two weeks, which, let me tell you, was not easy. You see the size of this thing?" Hazel gives the box a final shove before slamming the tailgate shut triumphantly.

When she finally turns to me, smiling, her bright, green eyes framed perfectly by her straight hair that's dyed some reddish-purple color, I have to force myself to look away. I hate that I still think she's the most beautiful thing I've ever seen. I nod toward the house, looking for a distraction. "Speaking of, where *is* mommy dearest?" The mere mention of her mother, Holly Blake, has a chill running down my spine.

"She's out at one of her *appointments*." Hazel makes air quotes with her fingers as she says that last part, making me think back to when we were teenagers. Any time Holly told us she had an appointment she would come home either freshly Botoxed and looking like her face got caught in a wind tunnel, or completely loopy and smelling like booze, as if she'd downed a handful of muscle relaxants and chased them with a bottle of scotch.

I relax against the car, leaning on the bumper. "I'm surprised you still live here. I thought you couldn't wait to escape this . . . what did you call it? The gilded birdcage from hell?" I crane my neck to look up at the enormous brick house, hating that I still know exactly which rain gutters to climb to get to Hazel's window.

Hazel shrugs. "My mom likes having someone else around and I kind of owe it to her. Plus it's not like I really have any place else to go." She points to the side building, which is the size of a small house. "But I live in the pool house apartment, so at least I have some sort of privacy."

I cross my arms and whistle. "All this and Mrs. B won't spring for a set of wheels, too?" I half-joke.

Hazel readjusts a bag slung over her shoulder. "Not for lack of trying, that's for sure. But it's bad enough I have to rely on her money to live here. I drew the line at her buying me a car, too. Some things I want to fix on my own, you know?" She smiles, but I can tell she's embarrassed.

I'm actually impressed by her seemingly sincere desire for independence, but since I'm trying not to think about things like that I simply opt to nod in agreement.

Hazel looks at me and I think she's going to say more, but she instead glances down the driveway before motioning toward my truck. "My mom should be back soon. We better get going."

We both get inside the truck and once we're seated Hazel turns to me. "Thanks for the ride, Tristan."

"I bet it won't be the last time I hear you say that." I grin suggestively and wink. A sick part of me can't resist being a dick, but an even sicker part of me hopes maybe it will scare her off, so we won't have to pretend with this whole "still friends" bullshit. I wasn't lying when I told her there's a lot I wish I could forget. The sooner she figures that out, the better. Right now I'm just giving her a ride to her brother's party, and that's it.

She just laughs, and the way it makes her face look like she's sixteen again makes my stomach sink. What in the actual fuck was I thinking, agreeing to this? We've barely spoken in five years and now we're going to be trapped alone in a car for thirty minutes?

Suddenly my oversized truck feels more like a cramped Smart Car.

CHAPTER

three

Hazel

CONTRARY TO POPULAR BELIEF, BEING locked alone in a car with the (former) love of your life for the first time in five years isn't as bad as it might seem. I really thought it would be completely awkward, but Tristan seems to be fine with it, so I am, too.

I'll be the first to admit it was weird to call him after so long. I mean, I'm well aware of the fact that I screwed things up, but that was a long time ago and it was a horrible time in my life . . . for many reasons. But I've been clean for over three years now and the more I try to get my life back on track, the more I haven't been able to get Tristan out of my head. I probably should have apologized for (or at least acknowledged) what I put him through, but as soon as I heard his voice on the other end of the phone it somehow felt easier to be *us* again. It's nice to pretend I have at least some piece of the only good thing I ever had in my life back, even if I don't deserve it.

As he makes his crude joke, I'm relieved to know Tristan hasn't lost his sense of humor. He was always a big flirt, and I'd be lying if I said it doesn't still give me some sort of thrill to hear his overtly sexual innuendos. If an average guy said the kinds of things Tristan Sharp gets away with, he would have a permanent handprint across his cheek from all the bitch slaps he'd no doubt be on the receiving end of.

But damn, there's something about Tristan that defies all logic.

Tristan concentrates on backing out of the driveway so I take the opportunity to study his face. It's been a long time since I've seen him this close.

He still has the same mess of short, dark hair that matches the sexy stubble covering his square jaw. And don't get me started on his smile . . . the one he gets when he's teasing you and bluntly says whatever the hell he thinks and you want to believe he's a moronic asshole but you actually find the fact he's so cocksure and unreserved impressive and amusing . . . *ugh*. I hate myself for loving it. How he manages to look adorable, smug, sexy, charming, *and* arrogant all at the same time I'll never truly understand, but it's infuriating how it makes my insides tingle with excitement.

I eye him curiously from my side of the car. While he physically looks the same as I remember, something is different about him. I can't quite put my finger on it.

Realizing I'm staring like a total creep, I instead look out my window. The sun is shining bright between the big white, fluffy clouds set against a clear blue sky. It's a perfect New England spring day.

We drive down the familiar streets of the neighborhood I've lived in my entire life, and as we pass our old high school I can't help but think about the past. A lot of bad has happened here, but some good was mixed in there, too. Wasn't there?

I'm suddenly all too aware of the silence in the car and I

have to remind myself to breathe. I've never been one for silence; it's always felt . . . overwhelming. It allows for too many things to flood my mind: thoughts, doubts, fears, truths. It might seem crazy, but for as long as I can remember I've found the quiet too loud; I often need noise to drown it out. At Greenside I learned to embrace the meditative quality of silence, but when I'm nervous the anxiety starts to kick in and I need something outside myself to focus on. It's either that or think about how much easier this would be if I were high right now.

I muse, "Can you believe my brother is getting married and having a kid?" As we drive down a few residential streets, colonial houses whiz by. Soon we'll cross into the commercial downtown area before getting on the highway.

"Pretty fucked up, if you ask me." Tristan shakes his head. "I never would have pegged him as a family man."

"Me neither." Another silence falls between us. "Speaking of relationships, was that your girlfriend I heard in the background when we talked last week?" The question comes out before I have time to think about it.

He chuckles and takes a right turn. "Not exactly."

I can't explain the feeling of relief that washes over me. I also can't help but be extremely interested to know everything that's been going on in Tristan's life. My questions become just as much a guilty pleasure as they are a distraction. "So, what have you been up to lately? Whenever I ask Ryan about you, he changes the subject."

"You ask about me, do you?" Keeping his eyes trained on the road, he gets a shit-eating grin on his face. *Way to play it cool, Hazel.*

I nonchalantly continue, "I heard you still work the same construction job you started in high school?"

Tristan drapes one hand lazily over the steering wheel and

takes a second before responding with a simple, "Yup."

I press on, hoping he will open up. "You must be good at your job if they kept you around this long."

"I guess."

Jesus, this is like pulling teeth. "Is Mr. Turner still running things?" I remember Tristan's boss from when we were in high school and I would meet Tristan at the construction site to hang out when he got off work.

"He's still around," Tristan says, glancing in the rearview mirror before switching lanes.

He clearly doesn't want to talk about himself, so I suppose I can be the first to share. "Well, right now I'm working as a waitress at the Crown Diner across town."

Tristan raises an eyebrow. "The one near the highway, between a motel and a strip club?"

I smirk. "It's a *gentleman's* club, but yup, that's the one."

"I'm surprised your mother would let you within five miles of that place, let alone work there." He sounds amused.

"She wouldn't, which is why she doesn't know. She'd rather remain oblivious than face something potentially embarrassing, so I figured it wasn't worth the argument to bring it up. Besides, I mostly work the late shift that starts at ten. It coordinates with the bus schedule so she probably doesn't even realize I'm gone, let alone wonder where I am."

Tristan's voice hardens and I notice his fingers grip the steering wheel a little tighter. "So you take the bus to some crappy, creepy-as-fuck diner in the middle of the night—all by yourself—and nobody even knows you're there?" He shakes his head incredulously.

When he puts it like that it makes me feel kind of stupid, but it really isn't a big deal. "I just told *you*, didn't I? Now somebody knows." I smile, trying to lighten the mood. Tristan looks only half amused so I shrug. "Hey, I'll take what I can get. It might not be the ideal place to work, but at least I'm good at it. I'm not exactly qualified to do much else, and it gives me some money to save until I can figure out what I really want to do with my life."

"You mean serving assholes pie at midnight isn't your dream job?"

I match his comical tone. "As fulfilling as it may be, eventually I think I'll want to branch out."

"Maybe take on the breakfast crowd, too?"

There he goes with that smile of his again. I can't help but laugh out loud. "I'd be damn good at it, I'm sure, but there's gotta be more to life than pancakes and eggs, right?"

"Like what?" he asks playfully.

"I don't know. I could be a nurse or something. Maybe work in a rehab facility and use my story to help people." I look out the window, suddenly uncomfortable. I've never admitted this idea out loud before, and I feel silly for thinking it could actually happen. When Tristan doesn't say anything, I feel even more ridiculous. "Yeah, it's stupid, I know." I flick an imaginary piece of lint from my jeans.

"I didn't say that. I just think it's an interesting tactic to use *your* life to help someone else's."

"What do you mean?" I tilt my head toward Tristan, genuinely curious.

He lifts his right shoulder lazily before letting it drop as he composes his thoughts. "I just think people spend too much time looking for some type of sympathy or validation or whatever else it is they think they gain from sharing every last detail of their lives. Focus on your own shit and don't burden other people with it. That's my take on it, anyway."

"I think most people are trying to feel connected. We all just want to be understood, right? And I've been through a lot, so why not share it in case someone can relate?"

"*Everyone's* been through shit—I promise we can all fucking relate to that. If you really want to help somebody, you need to make it about them, not you."

I open my mouth to zing him with some sassy comeback, but when I stop to think about it, Tristan makes a lot of sense. Sure, his delivery makes him sound like an inconsiderate asshole, but beneath all that he has a point. When I think back on everything we've been through together, I know that's exactly what he's always done . . . put me first. No matter what mess I got into, he never judged me or lectured me. He simply tried to save me from myself. Unfortunately, I was too selfish to see it at the time.

For a split second I consider opening up and letting him know everything I'm feeling, but talk about being selfish. After five years I can't dump all of my broken feelings on Tristan and expect him to pick up the pieces. Besides, I'm not here to live in the past or waste time on regrets, I just hope to gain back enough of his trust to call him a friend again. And OK, yes, that is still extremely selfish of me, but I'm only human!

I can remember the exact day three years ago that I was finally sober enough to realize I had made the biggest mistake of my life by letting Tristan Sharp walk out of it. I was in the common room at the Greenside Rehabilitation Center with my counselor and seven other recovering drug addicts, only a few weeks away from finishing my program and being released. The counselor asked us each to close our eyes and picture our future. The idea was to imagine where we wanted to be in five, ten, twenty years and use that as motivation to stay clean. People's dreams were all over the place, ranging from becoming a brain surgeon to having six kids, to going scuba diving in Costa Rica. When they got to me, though, no matter how hard I tried to picture anything else, the only thing I saw was Tristan's face. That's when I knew I was in trouble.

And now I'm playing with fire, craving time with him again. It must be the rebel in me that needs to push limits, even when I know it's a really bad idea. But trust me, it's my own kind of sick torture. I know I don't deserve anything Tristan might have to give me anymore. That ship has sailed and I basically doused it in kerosene before throwing a lit book of matches on it, only to stand there and watch it go up in flames before sinking right to the bottom of the Atlantic.

But here I am, trying to salvage any little piece I can, searching for something I don't even know how to name.

I clear my throat, trying to keep my voice from sounding as faraway as my mind. "Wow, that's pretty deep, Tristan."

As soon as the words are out of my mouth I realize how they sound. As expected, Tristan easily follows up with, "I bet it won't be the last time I hear you say that."

The richness of his voice causes dirty thoughts to fill my mind. I try not to blush and turn on the radio, needing a whole new kind of distraction.

CHAPTER

four

Hazel

A SHORT WHILE LATER WE pull up to a big house that I know is Eli Graham's. My brother is best friends with Eli's son, Lucas. Last year Lucas married Kinsley, who happens to be best friends with Kelley, my brother's baby momma. (You got all that?) Lucas and Kinsley are hosting the shower, and I'm excited to see everyone again. I was so worked up about being around Tristan I didn't have time to think about the whole reason for today. I still think it's nuts that my brother is going to be a dad (and that I'm going to be an aunt) but I really like Kelley. I met her a few months ago at my mother's annual Christmas party and I can tell Ryan adores her. I can also tell she doesn't take crap from anyone, which makes her my kind of girl.

As soon as I walk in with Tristan I can see that my brother is pissed. He knew we were both coming, just not *together*. When we were younger Ryan was always the overbearing big brother, threatening to beat up any guy that came near me. I know he thinks Tristan was somehow involved with everything that happened to me, but he refuses to ever talk about it. Since we've all grown up together and they're friends I didn't think it would still be such a sore spot. I wish I had the courage to tell Ryan the whole story, but it's too shameful to even think about.

It's extra awkward since Ryan has no idea that Tristan and I are more than familiar with each other, as I know that would be the final nail in Tristan's coffin. Talking about how his little sister lost her virginity to one of his closest friends isn't exactly a conversation to have with Ryan at the dinner table. Not that we ever had a normal family dining experience.

I love my brother, but he practically abandoned me as soon as he was old enough to get out of my mother's house. Sure he comes to visit occasionally, and while I know he is always there for me if I really need him, I still wish he were around more. First my dad left us when we were kids, and then Ryan left before I even turned eighteen. I'm proud of all he's accomplished, getting and staying sober and putting himself through school to become a successful lawyer. It all gives me hope that I, too, can break free from our messed-up past. But it also makes me sad to see everyone around me moving on while I seem to be stuck going nowhere.

As I walk up to Ryan to give him a hug he nods to Tristan, who is saying hello to Kelley. He doesn't even try to keep the disdain out of his voice. "What are you doing with him?"

I pull back, remembering that this is Ryan and Kelley's day, and try to keep the annoyance out of my own voice. "Do you know how hard it was to get out without Mom knowing where I was going? I needed a ride and called him. Don't give me that look, Ry. I'm not a kid anymore. By the way, Grams says she's sorry she can't make it, but I have a big gift from her in the car."

He's not thrilled, but at least he drops the subject. I'm able to give Kelley a quick hug before more people start to arrive, at which point I escape into the living room where I find Kinsley adjusting some white peonies in a yellow vase. I hear her floral design business, Petal, is doing really well, no doubt due to her extreme perfectionism. At my mom's last Christmas party, in between sulking because Tristan was avoiding me and watching drama unfold between Kelley and my mom, I talked to Kinsley for a bit. Once you get her started on talking flowers she really lights up.

"Hey Kinsley. The place looks great!" I lean in for a hug.

"Thanks, Hazel. I'm so glad you could make it." Kinsley smiles warmly and we hear loud voices across the room when more people arrive. Tristan makes his way over to us and wraps Kinsley in a giant bear hug.

"There's my favorite flower lady. When are you going to leave that shitty husband of yours and let me show you what being with a real man is like?" Tristan speaks loudly, so Kinsley's husband Lucas can hear him from the other end of the room, where he's leaning against the wall.

"Fuck you, Sharp," Lucas deadpans.

I laugh and exchange a hello nod with Luc.

Tristan grins, looking quite pleased to be causing trouble with his friends, while Kinsley blushes and slaps him playfully on the shoulder. I feel a hand tousle the top of my head.

"Hey, Zee."

I smile, instantly knowing who it is. Only one person calls me by that nickname and insists on messing up my hair every time he sees me. And he just so happens to be Tristan's twin brother. "Hey, Logan. Still mature as ever, I see." I try to smooth my hair back into place.

The twins eventually wander over to greet Lucas, and Kinsley and I watch them all joke and laugh as they catch up. Boys . . . how they can insult each other one minute and joke the next always amuses me. Having known my brother's friends most of my life, it's funny to see them now. While I've felt re-moved from their lives for the past decade, I can remember the four of them as a raunchy group of horny high-school boys, breaking hearts and causing trouble. Not that I was any better . . .

I can feel Kinsley's eyes on me as she asks, "So you came with Tristan, right? You two are close?"

I shrug, trying to conceal a guilty smile. *Close* doesn't even begin to describe the history between Tristan and me, but no-body else knows that. "I've known him since I was seven years old. And we went to high school together. We used to be good friends." I pick up a paper plate from the food table next to us and start to fill it. I'm not hungry, but I need something to keep my hands busy.

Kinsley nods and busies herself with rearranging some yel-low frosted cupcakes on the same table. When she doesn't follow up, I take the opportunity to fish for information. Tristan wasn't exactly forthcoming on our ride over, and since Lucas and Logan are business partners at their venture capital firm, GS Ventures, I assume Kinsley hears a lot about what goes on between the boys.

I add a few carrot sticks and two mini quiches to my plate. "You've been with Lucas for a while now, so you must know all the guys pretty well, too, right?"

Kinsley chuckles and licks some frosting off her thumb. "Yeah, you could say that. They're quite the bunch."

Not exactly the juicy tell-all I was hoping for. Maybe if I try a different approach? I don't exactly have many close girl-friends . . . or *any* friends, really, so I'm new to this whole gossip thing. "Tristan seems to adore you. Dare I say there might be a bit of history there?"

I go for nonchalant and playful, but I don't think it works. Kinsley looks shocked before her frown turns into a knowing smile. "You totally hooked up with him, didn't you?"

"Wh-what?" I stutter. "Of course not." My instinct is to deny this vehemently as I pile more vegetables, a handful of chips, and a big scoop of salsa on my plate.

Kinsley looks embarrassed and says, "Oh, my mistake. Sorry about that. I thought I caught a vibe, but I guess not."

I feel guilty for lying. It may be tempting to have another girl to talk to about this, but I don't think I'm ready to admit all the crazy feelings I still have for Tristan.

"Oh, please don't feel bad. Like I said, we used to be close, but really, we're just friends. If you can even call us that." I mutter that last part, but Kinsley hears it and looks confused. I quickly follow up, "I was just curious to know what Tristan has been up to since we don't see each other much now, that's all. He's hard to read."

Kinsey smiles. "Don't worry, I completely understand."

She doesn't press me to divulge any more information, which I'm grateful for. I look down at my paper plate, which is about ready to break under the weight of all the food piled on it. Good thing I'm not actually an emotional eater or I'd be as big as a beluga whale by now.

Feeling like I've already made a complete mess of this situation and of this entire day, I ask Kinsley where the ladies' room is. She points down the hall. I don't want her to see me throw away the giant plate of food I just made, so I take it with me as I shuffle to the bathroom and close the door, letting my head fall back against it.

After a few deep breaths I place the plate on the sink counter. I rest my hands next to it and bow my head.

What the hell are you doing, Hazel?

That is a very good question.

I feel the smooth ceramic tile under my fingertips and cringe when I picture myself doing lines off it. There would have been a time in my life when I would have come to a party to do just that. The feeling of complete, numbing ecstasy that allows you to forget anything exists is an experience that I hate to love.

I look at myself in the oval mirror above the faucet. The emerald shower curtain reflects behind me, making my green eyes glow. In rehab we were encouraged to explore why we turned to drugs in the first place, so I often think about how to describe it.

Have you ever had a dream where it felt so real you find yourself feeling sick that it's happening but you can't make it stop? And even though after you wake up it seems completely ridiculous and you want to cry in relief, in the dream it made complete sense? Well I guess that's how I felt growing up—like I was in some sort of bad dream where I knew I was making bad choices, but I couldn't stop myself. Except I never got to wake up, and it just kept getting worse. My father walked out when I was eight and my mother basically ignored Ryan and me after that—when she wasn't criticizing us, that is. We grew up with money and what would appear to be every advantage, but my life always felt empty. I just remember feeling depressed, anxious and alone. I was a no one who nobody cared about. As I got older, that feeling became overwhelming. In high school I became friends with some people who seemed to get that, and when they told me doing coke was easier than doing life, I believed them. I used to think not feeling anything was the only way to survive. Being high was the only time I felt both numb enough to deal with the pain and alive enough to continue living, and it became an addiction I didn't want to let go of for fear I would go back to being nothing.

But thankfully, after I denied I had a problem for far too long, my mom forced me into rehab and it changed my life. I've been clean and sober for three years now, although it's still a struggle every day.

"If you want to move beyond the past, you have to stop living in it," my counselor's voice echoes in my head.

Yeah, easier said than done, pal.

Between my cold reunion with Tristan and being here with so many former friends, I can't stop thinking about all the stupid crap I did in the past and how my life is somehow *still* a mess. And trying to cover it all up by lying makes me feel like an immature high schooler again, not a twenty-seven-year-old woman who is finally getting her shit together.

I grab a mini quiche from my plate and shove it in my mouth to distract myself. Not helping.

I scrape the rest of my plate into the toilet and flush.

At this point, I'm wishing I hadn't left my bag and phone in the other room. I could really use some music to blast right about now.

I sit on the edge of the tub and take a few more deep breaths: five seconds in, five seconds out. I focus on the present, on all the good in my life (something else my counselor would advise me to do). Finally I'm calm enough to realize that I'm lucky to be here, celebrating the new life my brother and Kelley are about to bring into this world. I may not have my life . . . or things with Tristan . . . figured out, but that's OK.

I just need to relax and take things as they come. I can't dwell on the past, but I can accept it.

I take another full breath before heading back out to the party.

You've got this, Hazel.

. . . Don't you?

CHAPTER
five

Tristan

I TRY TO FOCUS ON the story Logan is telling, but I can't seem to ignore the sick feeling in my stomach when I see Hazel bolt to the bathroom. It's a feeling I get only around her. I hate that my mind goes there.

I heard she went to rehab a few years back and I hope for her sake she's stayed clean, but I should no longer have any vested interest in whether it's true. She could be having a fucking party in the bathroom for all I care—which seems more than likely, judging from the mountain of food she brought with her.

Except I do care, which is why I never should have agreed to give her a damn ride. Out of sight, out of mind only works when the thing you're trying to forget is in fact out of sight, and not sitting in your fucking truck, right next to you, talking about things that you don't want to care about.

But I'll always care about Hazel Blake.

It's the thing I hate most about myself.

It's the thing that makes me hate *her*.

WHEN THE PARTY'S OVER A couple hours later I'm left in the living room with Ryan, Kelley, Lucas, Kinsley, my brother, and, of course, Hazel. When she finally came out of the bathroom earlier she looked noticeably calmer. *Don't think about why, T.* Other than that she seemed fine, smiling and laughing with some of the guests. She even took a camera out of her bag at one point, and thankfully became preoccupied with taking pictures.

I wouldn't say I'm avoiding her, but I'm not *not* avoiding her, either.

Now everyone is helping to clean up while Kelley and Ryan relax on the couch. It's obvious Kelley shouldn't be doing anything since she's eight months pregnant. Last I checked, Ryan isn't the knocked-up one. But still, he's stretched out, resting with his arms behind his head and his ankles crossed like a smug bastard. I saw the shitty look he gave me when I walked in with Hazel, and that makes me want to bust his balls.

As I continue to gather up assorted empty cups and plates from around the room I direct my glare to him. "Care to help, or are you just going to sit there like an asshole?" It's not unusual for me to give him crap, but even I'll admit that came out harsher than I intended. I guess I'm harboring some resentment that he continues to hate me for shit that happened years ago. I'm usually the first to play it cool, but everything with Hazel has me on edge.

Acting completely unfazed, he replies, "Nah, I'm good. But you missed some trash over there." He nods at the side table.

"Fuck you, princess. It's not like you're the pregnant one," I shoot back, picking up the dirty cup and crushing it in my hand before tossing it roughly into a trash bag.

"No, but he's half my kid, which means it's my party, too." Ryan stretches out further to make himself more comfortable, purposely egging me on, so I decide not to hold back with my thoughts on the whole subject. I know Ryan like I know my own brother, and ever since he told us he was engaged I've felt a weird vibe. While he is never one to openly talk about who he fucks, it's a well-known fact he's not the monogamous type. My current frustration and anger make me want to call him on it.

"Yeah, about that." I motion between Ryan and Kelley. "I still don't get it. Are you sure this isn't all a joke? Be honest with us, bro—you couldn't keep your dick in your pants and knocked her up by accident, didn't you."

"What the fuck, T?" Lucas jumps in.

I shrug. "What? I'm just saying, if you're not going to sack it, go home and whack it."

Everyone glares at me now, like I'm being the unreasonable asshole. I may be an asshole, but I'm not unreasonable. I do, however, see the scared look on Kelley's face, which I do feel bad about. I really don't have anything against her. This is meant to be between Ryan and me, so I attempt an explanation. "Come on, you have to admit this whole settling down thing is shady as shit. We all know Ry is a use 'em and lose 'em kind of guy, and then all of a sudden he's playing house with some random chick out of the blue?"

Shit, that didn't come out right either. Kelley looks even more humiliated. Fuck!

Before I have time to apologize Ryan is up, hands fisted at his sides. He gets in my face. "You don't know what the hell you're talking about, so I suggest you shut your goddamn mouth. It's none of your fucking business what I do or who I do it with, but if I ever hear you refer to Kelley as some random chick ever again I'll kick your fucking teeth in, like I should have done years ago."

Lucas and Logan move to separate us. I study Ryan's threatening glare before finally backing off. As much as it annoys the fucking shit out of me that he gets to blame me for what happened with Hazel, it's my choice. I know it would just upset him more to know the truth. I'd rather have him think I'm an asshole than know what really happened with his sister.

Ryan holds his hands up in surrender, indicating he's cool. He reaches for Kelley's hand and grinds out, "We're going." He pulls her to the front door, slamming it behind them.

"Really, Tristan? You had to bust his balls today of all days?" Lucas shakes his head then resumes stuffing a garbage bag.

"Whatever, man. He had it coming." I tie up my own full bag and toss it to the side while trying not to make eye contact with Hazel, who I know is staring at me.

THE RIDE BACK TO HAZEL'S has been quiet so far, which is unusual since she typically can't stand the silence. When we were younger she even needed music to fall asleep, and I find myself wondering if she still does. I almost ask, but stop myself. Taking a trip down memory lane won't do either of us any good. Thankfully, Hazel finally interjects.

"I'm sorry for what Ryan said to you . . . the part about how he should have kicked your ass years ago. I know that's my fault . . ."

Her voice trails off and my hands tense on the steering wheel. I know exactly what she's referring to. Anytime I think about what happened it makes me want to either puke or punch something. Sometimes both.

I shrug it off, hoping my voice sounds more relaxed than I feel. "I made a promise, didn't I?"

As I pull onto Hazel's street she adds, "And now I realize how selfish it was for me to have asked you to do that. Maybe it's time—"

I bring the truck to a quick stop on the side of the secluded road and throw it in park. I know what she's going to say, but there is no way in hell that telling Ryan the truth right now is going to make things better. It's not going to change the past and I have no interest in opening old wounds. "I'm going to stop you right there. What happened, happened. It's in the past and that's where it's going to stay. Trust me, Hazel, nothing good will come from rehashing things." I cut the ignition. We planned for me to drop her off a few doors down from her house in case her mother is home, and I'm relieved we don't have the whole car ride home to talk about this.

"I just want you to know how much your help means to me, Tristan. How much *you* mean to me."

When I see the way Hazel looks gratefully at me with those big, sexy green eyes my relief turns to panic and I suddenly wish I had something else to focus on. I silently curse the fact we're just sitting here. Not moving. Alone. In my truck. On a quiet, secluded street with Hazel looking all sorts of vulnerable and tempting in her form-fitting red T-shirt and tight jeans.

I equally curse my dick, who, judging from the fact that he's chosen this moment to wake up, has also noticed the way Hazel's shirt stretches across her perfectly rounded breasts.

In this moment I wonder if the past really can be the past and we can start over. If there is even the slightest chance of us ever being *us* again. I want to know if her body would still feel like fire under my fingertips. If her lips would still taste as earthy and sweet. If she would still lock her eyes on mine the moment I bury myself inside her.

I slowly lean in, trying to breathe in her light, citrusy scent. It's hard to put what she smells like into words except for what I can only describe as sunshine and fucking rainbows. She licks her lips and inhales, lifting her head ever so slightly to meet mine.

I'm so close I'd barely have to move to taste her. I move my eyes from her full, pink lips to her deep, dangerous eyes and suddenly my desire is replaced with something I can't identify. Resentment? Mistrust?

Rather than let myself get sucked into what could only be a very bad fucking idea, I instead whisper, "Goodnight, Hazel," before pulling back.

I smile casually to mask how affected I am by this girl. I knew it was a mistake to let her back into my life. The sooner I shut this down, the better.

I try to read Hazel's reaction, but she simply smiles back and lets herself out of the car. Before she closes it she leans in, giving me the most perfectly frustrating view right down the front of her shirt. "Goodnight, Tristan. Remember, I owe you a ride." She winks and slams the door, leaving me to watch her walk away.

As soon as she disappears around the corner I bang my hands against the steering wheel, needing to vent some of this unexpected pent-up tension. I'm both pissed I was tempted to give in and pissed I stopped myself. I take a minute to compose myself before turning the key in the ignition. Right before I put the truck in drive, I dial Logan's number on my cell.

As soon as I hear the call pick up I don't even let him speak before commanding, "Dude, get your ass over to my place—we're going out. I need to get laid ASAP." I end the call, toss my phone into the passenger seat, and peel out as fast as I can. The farther I can get away from Hazel Blake, the better.

CHAPTER

Tristan

AN HOUR LATER I'M AT Chaser's with Logan, already knocking back my second beer. This bar is our usual place when we just want to chill and unwind, maybe have a little fun. It's a dive bar with low lighting, an old-school jukebox, and a pool table in the back. It may not be the classiest of places, but it's not a dump, either. Right on the outskirts of the main downtown strip, it's the kind of bar you come to after a long day of work, knock back a cold beer, and find someone to take your mind off of whatever shit you might be going through.

Speaking of, a busty brunette appears at my right elbow. She surveys me with a predatory look and nods to my bottle. "Care to buy a girl a drink?" She licks her lips and pushes her tits closer to my arm, staring me down like a piece of meat. Normally I'd find this behavior ballsy enough to interest me, but tonight I just find it lame.

"I'm good." I barely make eye contact and focus my attention in the opposite direction as she walks away. Part of me feels bad for being such an asshole about it, but then I see she's already fixated on her next victim, so fuck feeling guilty.

Logan eyes me as he takes a swig from his own bottle of Sam Adams and laughs to himself.

"What?" I ask, irritated.

"Nothing. Lucas owes me a hundred bucks is all."

"What the hell are you talking about?"

He takes another drink from his beer before tilting it toward the brunette who's hitting on some other poor bastard across the room. "I've never seen you turn down an easy opportunity like that, and I assume it's because of a certain someone you escorted to the party earlier." He shakes his head and grabs a handful of peanuts from the small bowl on the bar. "That girl has always fucked with your head, so I made a little wager."

My brother looks downright smug since he thinks he's nailed me, his signature dimples on full display. We might be twins, but he's the lucky asshole that won the genetic lottery. He's a smooth talker—in perfect contrast to my often-blunt attitude—so between the charm, the dimples, and his dirty blond hair, girls practically throw their underwear at him. We usually make an irresistible lady-killing team, but sometimes he just annoys the shit out of me. "Fuck you, bro. Hazel has nothing to do with anything. Can't a guy just enjoy a beer in peace?"

Logan laughs. As a general rule we share everything—DNA, secrets, women—but this is one of the few things I don't want to discuss. He may not know the full story about Hazel, but he knows me well enough not to buy my crap.

"Come on, T. What's up? Something—or should I say some-one—is clearly bothering you. First you start shit with Ryan, well, more shit than usual anyway, and you've been zoned out since we got here. You didn't even notice your favorite smokeshow by the door."

I turn around to rest my elbows back on the bar and look out around the room. An upbeat song pumps through the jukebox speakers. I see Tiffany standing by the entrance with a group of friends, sizing me up from the corner of her eye. Petite. Blonde. Perfect rack to ass ratio. Hot, and knows it. We've fucked a few times and normally on a night like this I'd have her back at my place already. Shit. Maybe Logan is right—maybe something *is* wrong with me. And I'll be damned if I let that fucker be right. I would take a bullet for the guy, but I'll cut off my own dick before I have to hear him give me shit about a girl.

Especially if it's about a certain girl I wish I could forget altogether.

I finish off the last of my beer and put the empty bottle on the bar behind me. I look back at Tiffany and we make eye contact before her gaze slides lower. I know my tanned arms and lean muscles are on full display in my gray T-shirt—perks of working outside on construction sites every day. Her eyes make their way back to mine so I flash her my usual charming smile. When she returns it with her own cutesy grin I honestly feel nothing, but I'd rather make meaningless conversation with some random fuck buddy than have my brother ask any more questions about Hazel.

I clap Logan on the back and motion to the bartender for two more beers. "You worry too much. What, are you on your period today? Relax."

Logan grunts as the cold bottles are placed in front of me. "Screw you, T. You're the one who's been bitchy all night. No wonder everyone thinks I'm the better brother." He laughs. "Instead of trying to get pussy, you're being one."

He reaches for one of the beers but I pull them both away. "That's about to change, brother." I grin cockily and head toward the blonde at the door, thankful that Logan and I each drove our own vehicles here tonight—something we usually do for this very reason. "Don't wait up," I call back, and hear an approving chuckle in response.

As soon as I get close to the group of girls I'm hit with an overpowering stench of perfume that makes me dizzy. It collectively smells like baby powder and strawberries mixed with tequila and a hint of desperation. I think of how Hazel had such a nice, subtle smell earlier and find myself feeling steadier as I wonder what it was. Orange? Lime? *Fuck.*

As if to prove a point to myself I move in closer to Tiffany. I drape my right arm over her shoulder from behind, offering her one of the beer bottles. "You look thirsty," I whisper in her ear before moving around to face her.

She smiles and accepts the drink, moving away from her friends to give me her undivided attention. "Thanks." She takes a slow sip before adding suggestively, "However can I repay the favor?"

"I'm sure we can think of something." Damn, this is almost too easy. Part of me wants to ask if she has any sort of self-respect. Not that I've ever cared before. She's wearing skin-tight black jeans and some sort of shimmery tank top that changes color every time she moves in the dim lights, forcing me to stare at her chest like two giant disco balls. I'm going to go with a 'no' on the whole self-respect thing.

I down a huge gulp of my own beer, hoping it will keep me from feeling so edgy, but by the way every vein in my body pulses with adrenaline I don't think it will help. I'm by no means a lightweight—it usually takes at least four beers before I even feel a buzz—but I don't think I should be consuming more alcohol when I feel drunk already. And not in a nice, relaxed way.

I contemplate getting the hell out of here, but then that means something really is wrong with me.

"So, how've you been?" Tiffany asks, but by the way she

stares at my muscles instead of making eye contact, I can tell she doesn't really care. I shrug, trying to keep my shit under control. My arms and legs feel hollow but I'm so wired I could run a marathon.

I'm well aware that most girls see me as nothing but a tool with a ripped body, and that's usually fine by me. I prefer it, actually, and the joke's on them, if you really think about it. The girls that end up in my bed tend to prowl bars, parties, and clubs, looking for attention from anyone who will give it to them. They only want to use me to make themselves feel better, which is fine since that's all I'm looking for. I see the way they look at me—at my abs and my dick, but never really at *me*—as they use me for their own sick pleasure, and this makes it easy for me to do the same. If a girl wants to use me for a night of fun, why not make the most of it? People can think what they want about me but I'm just enjoying the ride, tickled fucking pink that I don't have to answer to or worry about anyone else.

I put my half-full beer bottle down on a table beside us and hook my thumb toward the door. "Let's get out of here. You want a ride?" To hell with making meaningless small talk. We both know what we're really after, so let's cut to the chase.

"Thanks for the ride, Tristan." I see Tiffany's lips moving, but I hear Hazel's voice in my head. I shake it to regain focus.

"I'm sorry, what?" I ask, praying I'm not having a nervous breakdown.

Tiffany slides closer to me, tracing the hem of my shirt with her finger. "I said, where do you want to go, handsome?" My body tenses at the way she looks at me. Not in a good way. *Come on, T. Get your thumb out of your ass and your head in the game.*

"Outside. Let's get some air." I motion to the side entrance that I know leads to an alley.

As soon as the fresh air hits my lungs and replaces the stale, stuffy feeling from inside the bar, I make my move. I push Tiffany up against the wall, caging her in with my arms. The cool concrete feels solid under my fingers, giving me the grounding I need. I angle my head to look at her, her short stature no match for my six-foot frame. She grinds her hips toward mine, her chest heaving with excitement. For the first time I notice that her eyes are green, which makes me think of Hazel's soft, sweet face.

"Fuck!" I groan, backing off.

Tiffany flinches, startled. "What? What's wrong?"

I squeeze my eyes shut and press my thumb and forefinger over them before blinking a few times, desperate to un-see the feisty redhead fucking with my mind. I look back at Tiffany and command, "Go back inside. I can't do this tonight."

She sticks out her unnaturally plump bottom lip in a pout before looking at me like I'm some sad puppy dog. "Aww . . . don't feel bad. It happens to a lot of guys. He probably just needs a little encouragement. Here, let me help." She reaches for the front of my jeans.

Jesus, she thinks I can't fucking get it up? If only that were my problem. I might prefer it at this point. My ego still takes a hit, though, so I throw my hands up defensively while putting as much distance between us as I can.

"That's not the problem. Can't you take a fucking hint?" I bite out harshly.

Now Tiffany is the one who looks offended. She crosses her arms and hisses, "Screw you, Tristan," before turning on her heel to stalk back inside.

I take a few deep breaths and pace the narrow alley before screaming "FUCK!" loudly into the night. I punch the concrete wall hard enough for my knuckles to bleed. I welcome the physical pain because it sure as shit beats the throbbing in my chest that started the minute Hazel Blake stormed back into my life.

CHAPTER

seven

Hazel

IT'S BEEN THREE HOURS SINCE Tristan dropped me off and I don't think I've sat still once. I'm so amped up from our almost-kiss that I think I might spontaneously combust. It took every ounce of my composure to casually walk away from his car. I could have sworn we both felt our old spark again, but by the way he shut me down I probably imagined it. Either way, I know I deserve the rejection.

As soon as I knew I was out of sight, I practically sprinted up to the pool house, locking the door as I leaned against it, my heart racing. I blasted loud music then spent a good hour pacing, got ready for work way too early, paced some more, and now I'm raiding my cabinets, since I never did eat at the party. I look from one empty shelf to another and curse when I realize I'm going to have to go up to the main house. I look at the clock, seeing I still have some time before I need to catch the bus to make it for my usual 10 p.m.—3 a.m. shift at the Crown.

I let myself in the back door that leads straight into the kitchen, trying to be quiet as I open the fridge and look for a snack. As soon as I grab an apple from the crisper drawer I hear a loud voice.

"Hazel, is that you?"

I jump, slamming the door shut with more force than I anticipated. "Jeez, Mom, you scared the shit out of me!" I clutch the apple to my chest, trying to calm down. Nothing like a jolt of adrenaline to make the already on-edge girl feel like she's having a heart attack.

My mother clicks her tongue. "Oh for goodness sake, Hazel, watch your language. And maybe you wouldn't be so jumpy if you weren't sneaking around like a cat burglar in your own home. Why on God's green earth are you wearing all black like some sort of hoodlum?"

I look down to my dark yoga pants and zip-up sweatshirt that's pulled over a T-shirt of the same color. The diner requires all waitresses to wear black and I like to be comfortable during my shift. It's not like I expect to meet anybody worth dressing up for in the middle of the night. Although apparently my mother does, since she's sporting a silk dressing gown with matching high-heeled slippers that have some sort of fluffy feathers attached to the top.

"What? It's comfortable." I shrug, opting for a half-truth. I really don't feel like arguing about my choice of employment right now.

She shakes her head, clearly unable to comprehend my logic, before sashaying to the sink to fill a glass with filtered water. "Where were you this afternoon? I came looking for you when I got home but you weren't here."

I rest my hands on the large marble island in front of me, spinning the apple on the smooth countertop to keep my hands busy. In rehab we learned that secrets, no matter how big or small, are a gateway drug—keeping them only leads to worse things. And while I understand that, I also know my mother. She has such a warped sense of reality that sometimes it's better to keep her in the dark. Besides, Ryan is the one who made me swear not to tell her about the baby shower, and as much as I might owe my mother for getting me into rehab, I don't want to make things worse between them. Ry and Mom have always butted heads, and she's not exactly thrilled with his choice of fiancée at the moment. Although I have to admit it was amusing to watch his soon-to-be-wife go toe to toe with my mom the night of the holiday party . . . I've never seen anyone do that but my brother. Ryan and Kelley are like a match made in Holly Blake-Hating Heaven.

"I was visiting with an old friend." *Not exactly a lie . . .*

My mother takes a sip of her water before getting to her real point. I should have known she doesn't actually care where I was. "I had lunch with Mrs. Brattelboro today and she told me her son has been asking about you. You remember Thomas, don't you?"

In ninth grade Tommy Brattelboro offered me a hundred bucks to show him my boobs. He's kind of hard to forget.

I nod, once again deciding to omit certain details from this conversation.

"Well I told her she should have him call you. I think he's quite the catch."

I groan and try not to roll my eyes. "Thanks, but no thanks."

My mom sets her glass on the counter and sighs dramatically. "I don't know why you have to be so difficult. You should consider yourself lucky a boy like Thomas Brattelboro takes the time to ask about you. He's a respected man with a good job. Not like poor Mitsy Hamilton's son, Jackson. I heard he's quite the drunk and went to rehab three times in as many years." She shakes her head in pity and I have to resist the urge to scream. It's bad enough I have to listen to her ridiculous gossip, which serves no purpose other than her own sick form of entertainment, but the judgment in her tone makes me cringe.

"Mom, *I've* been to rehab. And your son used to be a drunk, too, remember?"

She waves a dismissive hand. "Don't be dramatic. I'm talking about Jackson Hamilton, not you. That boy is real trouble."

Oh my God. The way this woman is able to ignore what she doesn't want to see is impressive. No wonder I used to prefer being high to dealing with her crap. She's always been more concerned about appearances than truth, but I'm starting to think she actually believes the lies she tells herself.

I suddenly get a bad feeling in the pit of my stomach. Maybe I'm more like my mother than I think. After all, haven't I tried to rewrite the past and lie to myself when it comes to Tristan? I guess I tried to pretend I didn't treat him like complete garbage all those years ago so we could forget it ever happened and go back to being friends. But he also made it pretty clear he doesn't want to talk about the past, either. So what was I supposed to do?

I argue, "If someone makes a mistake, that doesn't mean they're a bad person." I'm no longer just talking about Jackson. I add in a softer, more hopeful tone, "We all have our flaws, but people can change, right?"

My mother laughs. "Oh, Hazel." She comes around the side of the island to stroke my hair in what I assume is meant to be an affectionate gesture, but feels patronizing. "A flaw is a weakness for a reason, my dear. Those who suffer bring it upon themselves."

With that uplifting nugget of motherly advice, she air kisses me on the forehead and makes her exit. As she heads through the doorway she calls over her shoulder, "Just remember, a leopard doesn't change its spots."

STEP ONE: HONESTY

We admitted that we were powerless over our addiction, that our lives had become unmanageable.

CHAPTER
eight

Tristan

"YO, TRISTAN! DID YOU HEAR me?"

Shit. "What?"

"I asked if you have the plans for the house over on Collins Street? I need to get some guys over there this week or Old Lady Buress is going to cut my dick off and feed it to her fucking Chihuahua."

I focus on measuring the same length of two-by-four for the eighteenth time as CJ looks at me expectantly. "Fuck, I forgot them at the office. I'll bring them tomorrow."

CJ laughs, so I look up from my tape measure and carpenter pencil. "Now what?"

He crosses his arms and leans against my makeshift workbench, which is a piece of plywood propped up on two sawhorses. "Nothing, except that's what you've been telling me for the past three days. Kinda makes my job as foreman on this one hard when I don't even have the blueprints. What's up, man?"

I toss my pencil on the bench and place my hands flat on the wood surface. I drop my chin to my chest and take a deep breath to clear my mind. It's been ten days since I last saw Hazel, and it's pissing me the fuck off that I can't get her out of my head.

Even more concerning is that it's been more than ten days since I've gotten laid, and the longest I've gone without sex in the past three years is five days. Six, tops, if I double down with some solo hands-on action. But ten? It must be the stress of a busy workweek. No way the mere thought of Hazel Blake has me cock-blocked.

I roll my shoulders to try and shake off whatever the fuck is wrong with me. "I've just got a lot going on. Too much to do and not enough time in the day to do it."

"Is that why you've been working from four in the fucking morning 'til it's darker than hell? I'm all for putting in hours, man, but damn, you might wanna ease up a bit. You're starting to look like shit. Well, even worse than usual."

Busting my balls is nothing new for CJ, since we've worked at Charter Hill Construction together going on eleven years, but right now I'm not in the mood. "Well somebody has to make sure this shit gets done," I snap, my usual joking tone replaced by a frustration even I don't understand. Usually I'm the most easy-going guy there is. Why the fuck is everyone annoying me lately?

CJ looks shocked at my unusual outburst and holds his hands up in surrender just as Mr. Turner approaches with a blue cardboard tube in his hands.

"Watch out for this one today, sir; somebody has his hot-pink panties in a twist." CJ laughs, thinking he's funny shit.

Mr. Turner shakes his head, used to our constant ribbing, and holds out the tube to CJ. "I saw this back at the office and thought you might need it. Now why don't you make yourself useful and get to work, huh?"

"With pleasure, Mr. T. At least *somebody* is paying attention." CJ shoots me a shit-eating grin before heading off the job site.

I try to get back to measuring this damn two-by-four as Mr. Turner comes around the opposite side of the workbench. He stays quiet, observing me, which is how I know I'm in trouble. Ben Turner is the kind of guy who doesn't have to say anything to get you to admit to something. He's been the closest to a father figure I've had in my life, and other than Logan I consider him my only family. He's the one person I try not to disappoint.

"I know I dropped the ball. It won't happen again." I don't look up from what I'm doing.

"Hey, it's your ball to drop. No need to explain it to me, son." Mr. Turner puts his hands in his pockets and for a second I think I'm in the clear.

"*But . . .*"

Fuck.

" . . . CJ is right. You do look like hell."

"Good thing I'm not trying to impress anyone," I grunt, finally looking up. "Look, I'm doing the best I can. I'm sorry if it's not up to your standards, but every project is on schedule, isn't it?"

"You don't have to answer to me anymore, remember? You're the boss now. When I sold you this company I had no doubts you could handle it. Sure you've always been a pain in my ass, but you're smart. Why you don't let anyone see that is beyond me, but judging from the books, you are more than capable of running things around here." He narrows his eyes at me, looking concerned. "But I also know what it's like to have this job consume you if you let it, and I don't want to see that happen to you."

I think about how working here is the only thing I've ever been proud of—or good at—and how all it took was one afternoon with Hazel to turn it to shit. She tends to have that effect on my life.

"Trust me, this job isn't the problem."

"Well then I doubt you're going to find the solution here, either. Why don't you go home and get some rest. Take the time to deal with whatever it is you need to. I don't want to see you put yourself or anyone else in danger by being too stubborn to admit it's time to take a break."

He claps me on the shoulder and I want to argue, but considering I've barely slept more than three hours a night for the past week, I really do need to get my shit under control. I need to find a way to forget what happened after the baby shower so I can move on.

In fact, I need to find a way to forget Hazel Blake altogether.

Eleven years ago

"TELL ME SOMETHING BEAUTIFUL."

"Something beautiful."

She nudges me playfully in the arm. "Come on, pleeease?"

Even though I know she's only asking something so ridiculous because she's high, I can't resist her begging. "Well what kind of beautiful thing do you want to hear about?"

"I don't know. Tell me a love story."

"Like Romeo & Juliet or some shit?"

"No, that one is too sad."

"But that doesn't mean it's not beautiful. It might not end so well, but it's still about two people who would rather die together than live apart. So yeah, that's sad, but you can't tell me that's not also fucking beautiful."

She gets quiet for a second. "I once heard this story about a man who was in an accident and lost his memory and couldn't remember anything about his life. His wife never gave up on him, though, and he ended up falling in love with her all over again. I think that's both sad and beautiful, too."

"Shit, that's even worse than Romeo & Juliet. I can't imagine what kind of hell it must be to wake up one day and forget who you are. Or who anyone else is."

"I bet you'd miss me if you couldn't remember me." She giggles.

I know she won't remember this conversation in the morning. I answer honestly anyway. "Yeah, I would."

We're lying on our backs, looking up at the stars. A moment of silence passes between us before she sits up and rummages in her bag. "Take off your shirt," she commands.

"Looking to take advantage of me?" I lift my eyebrows, but pull my shirt over my head.

"Now lie back."

I do as she asks. "A guy could get used to this." I place my arms behind my head and close my eyes.

She laughs and gets closer. Instead of her climbing on top of me, I feel a soft, scratching sensation on my chest.

I look down and see her scribbling something with a black permanent marker.

I try to lift my head to make out what she's doing but she shields it from my view with her free hand. "No peeking."

She bites her lip and seems to be concentrating really hard. Maybe I should be concerned about what she's doing, but all I can think about is how sexy she looks while doing it.

When she's finished she sits back on her knees and studies her work. "Perfect."

I crane my neck and look down at my bare skin. It takes me a second before I make out what it says.

Hazel was here.

She puts her hand over my heart, tracing the lines she just made.

"There. Now even if you lose your memory, you won't ever be able to forget me."

I jolt out of bed, not sure if I should be grateful or irritated. It's bad enough every waking thought has been consumed by Hazel, but when I finally get to sleep I have to dream about our past together, too?

I look at the clock: 1:47 a.m. Awesome.

I head to the bathroom and lift up my shirt to make sure there are no black marks there. You know, just in case.

I shake my head and splash some water on my face. As I pat my skin dry with a towel I notice my reflection. Damn, I really do look like shit. Barely sleeping, showering, or shaving for over a week will do that to a guy. The last time I looked like this . . . well, I guess that would be about five years ago. Damn. Who the fuck am I?

My high-school self was right—losing yourself is the worst kind of hell.

I stare at myself in the mirror. Maybe this is who I once was, but it sure as hell isn't who I am now. There is no way Tristan Sharp is going to lose himself over some chick. I made that mistake once before, letting Hazel Blake consume every part of me until she left me empty and lifeless. It took me a long time to learn not to give a fuck about feelings when it comes to women and I'm sure as shit not going to stop now.

So maybe I'm still attracted to Hazel. So what? That just shows I'm a normal guy reacting to a hot girl. There doesn't have to be any sort of deeper meaning than that. It'd actually be weirder if I *didn't* want to bone her. Sex is just sex.

And OK, there are about a million other reasons why I shouldn't go there, the fact that her brother would rip my balls off and beat me with them being pretty high on that list. Ryan already hates me in any way that involves his sister, so it's probably not in my best interest to fuel that fire.

But then again, I've always liked to live dangerously.

If I've learned one thing after being with the number of women I've hooked up with, it's that sex is all about power, so if I let Hazel get in my head and mess with my ability to fuck, then she wins. And there is no way I am going to let that happen. As long as I stay in control I can prove once and for all that all I need to put this shit to bed is to get Hazel into one. That's all I need to get her out of my system for good.

I tear off my clothes and jump in the shower, washing away all the dirt, sweat, and memories of the past week and a half. I shave and throw on a pair of clean jeans and a fresh black T-shirt. I grab my keys from the kitchen counter, hop in my truck, and head across town. Suddenly, I think I'm in the mood for pie.

Hey, if I can't forget Hazel Blake, I might as well fuck her.

CHAPTER

nine

Tristan

I PARK ON THE DESERTED, dimly lit street in front of the Crown Diner. It's one of those classic 24-hour joints with chrome fixtures, a black-and-white checkered floor, and a too-bright neon sign that flickers sporadically. Outside the club across the street, a few drunken guys stumble around. The thought of Hazel working here still bothers the shit out of me, but I don't read too much into it. Hell, I'm freaked out to be here in the middle of the night myself. I don't like the idea of *any* girl having to work here.

As soon as I walk up to the glass door I recognize the waitress behind the register. She's leaning over the narrow back counter, refilling salt and pepper shakers, and even though her back is to me I can tell it's Hazel.

My gut instinct is to turn right back around and get the fuck out of Dodge, but I know I have to get her out of my system if I have any chance of putting her behind me, so I instead force myself to focus on how great her ass looks in a pair of black yoga pants. Yeah, I'm a real martyr, I know.

I pull open the door and as soon as I'm inside Hazel calls

out, "Feel free to sit anywhere you'd like." Without looking up she raises her left hand to motion around the empty restaurant, still pouring salt into one of the glass shakers with her right. "Do you need a menu or do you know what you're in the mood for?"

"I happen to know exactly what I'm in the mood for."

Hazel whips around, knocking over one of the salt shakers. "Tristan? Oh my God, what the hell are you doing here?"

Her hand moves over her chest. She looks shocked to see me. And maybe a little thrilled?

"I was in the neighborhood." I shrug coolly.

She gives me a doubtful look, regaining her composure. "At three in the morning?"

"Is that what time it is?" I slide onto one of the bar stools at the counter and pick up a menu, pretending to look it over without a care in the world.

I can feel Hazel studying me. "I thought you said you knew what you wanted?" she asks in a playful tone.

I flash her a knowing smile. "It's always good to keep your options open."

She rolls her eyes, but I can tell she's amused. "What are you really doing here?" She rests her hands on the counter in front of me. I catch a whiff of that same damn citrusy smell and have to remember to keep my cool.

Even though we're the only two around, I lean in closer so only she can hear. "Maybe I decided we should finish what we started in my truck last week."

Without missing a beat, she tries to call me out. "So you're here for a booty call? What, your giggly friend from the other week isn't available?"

Damn, that's the Hazel I remember: feisty as hell. I lean back, talking at a normal volume again. "I think we can both agree there's some unfinished business between us. Can you really say you don't miss me?"

Hazel smirks, but before she can answer the diner door opens and a tall, middle-aged woman with curly black hair comes rushing in. "Hey girly. Can't believe I made it here in time. I stayed up way too late watching The Bachelor reruns and almost missed my alarm." The woman heads behind the counter and begins tying on an apron. "I thought for sure I'd be late and Chet would dock my pay again."

"I think you're good, Nan. It's been dead here so he's been in the office all night watching something on the television back there." Hazel moves away from me, takes an order pad from her apron and places it under the register.

"I'm sure I can guess what he's watching." The woman shudders. "Gross."

Hazel laughs and checks the big clock on the back wall. "Good luck with him. I should get going so I don't miss the bus, though."

I interrupt as Hazel unties her own apron. "I can give you a ride."

Both women look at me before Hazel raises a quizzical eyebrow. "You haven't even ordered yet."

"Turns out I'm craving something other than diner food." I smile suggestively.

The woman puts a protective hand on Hazel's shoulder while giving me a dirty look, but before she can say anything Hazel clarifies, "Don't worry, he's an old friend. Nan, this is Tristan, Tristan, this is my coworker, Nancy, but everyone calls her Nan."

Nan puts her hand to her chest and lets out a sigh of relief. "Good thing. I was about to kick his perverted behind right out the door." She turns her attention to me, giving me a skeptical once-over. "I don't care how good looking you are, sugar, nobody messes with my girl here."

"And what about you? I'm sure you have to beat guys off with a stick, don't you?" I flash Nan my most charming grin.

She shoos the thought away as if I'm crazy, but by the way she blushes I can tell it's helping to win her over. It's true she's not exactly MILF status, but every woman appreciates a little flirting. And if there is one thing that helps to make me feel like my usual, unaffected self, it's definitely some shameless flirtation.

I stand up and notice Hazel seems unsure. She looks at me, then at the door, then back at me before asking, "Are you sure you don't mind? I still have time to catch the bus."

Am I sure? Fuck no. "I offered, didn't I?" Realizing that sounded harsher than I intended, I follow up with a wicked smile. "If it makes you feel better you can owe me."

"Mmm, honey if you don't take him up on his offer, I might," Nan cuts in and winks at me.

"Well look who no longer thinks I'm a pervert. Better hurry, Hazel, or you two will have to fight over me."

Hazel laughs. "Just let me grab my stuff." She disappears into the back for a few seconds before returning with a sweatshirt folded over her arm and a bag slung over her shoulder. "Ready?" she asks, nodding toward the door.

Isn't that a good fucking question.

CHAPTER

ten

Hazel

"READY?" I ASK, NOT SURE exactly what I'm referring to: leaving the diner or seeing what's going to happen once we do.

Tristan nods, holding the door open. He leads me to his truck parked just outside.

To say I was surprised to see him at this hour in the first place would be a major understatement, but to have him basically proposition me for sex has me feeling all kinds of confused. When I saw him last he seemed quiet and distant, like we were practically strangers, but now it's like we're back to being friends. On the one hand I feel like something is up and I should ask him what's going on, but on the other I can't help but be grateful for anything he's willing to give me as long as it means I get to spend time with him. And yes, I'm aware just how sad and desperate that makes me, but that doesn't stop me, either. If there is any chance I might have another shot with Tristan Sharp, I'll do whatever he wants.

As I approach the truck Tristan gets close, brushing past me to open my door. It's still dark and the early morning air has a chill, but I don't think that's why goose bumps suddenly flush my entire body. I climb into the passenger seat and wait anxiously for him to move around to the driver's side. He gets in, secures his seatbelt, and pulls onto the road.

"Thank you for taking me home," I say, needing to break the silence.

"Sure that's where you want me to take you?"

I angle myself as best I can with the restraint of the seatbelt to face him. As much as I want this to be like old times, I need to know where his head is really at. "What was with all that stuff you said at the diner? Were you just messing with me?"

His eyes flick over to me before focusing back on the road. "Do you really think I came all the way out here at this hour to mess with you?"

I think about it for a second. "I don't know, Tristan. I don't know anything about you anymore."

"There isn't much to know."

We're both quiet for a moment before he sighs and adds, "Sure, we've been through some shit together. That's life, though. I have no interest in bringing any of that up, but spending time together made me remember there was at least one area of our relationship we were good at." He raises his eyebrows with a knowing smirk. "Come on, haven't you wondered what it would be like to get me in the sack again after all this time?"

I could try denying it, but really, what would be the point? "And if I have?" I suck in a breath.

His voice is low, yet light. "Then what would you say to satisfying both of our curiosities?"

Without giving myself a chance to think I command, "I'd say pull the truck over."

Tristan looks at me with a mixture of surprise and lust and stops the truck a few feet off the side of the road. We're on a dark, secluded street and, considering the time, I doubt many cars will come through this way. But still, the thrill of possibly getting caught mixes with the thrill of what I think is about to happen and makes my heart drum inside my chest, the vibration shooting down between my legs, leaving me wanting and wet.

Tristan leans over the center console, getting so close that I can smell his clean and earthy scent. I still remember when he would come to see me after working all day at his construction job, dirty and smelling of sweat and soil. It's a scent that is so distinctly Tristan that I can't help but be consumed by it.

His lips ghost over mine. "This is just sex, Hazel, for old time's sake. Nothing more. You can handle that, right?"

His brown eyes blaze into my green ones and I swear he can read every single thought racing through my mind. I'm not sure I can handle anything when it comes to Tristan Sharp these days, but I do know I don't want to have to think about it right now. My desire overtakes all judgment and I feel myself nod. Tristan whispers, "Good," right before his tongue slides down my neck.

Suddenly it's like we're back in high school. No words are needed as our bodies fall into a familiar rhythm, except what I remember as slow and unhurried now becomes fast and frantic. Within seconds the driver's seat is pushed back and I'm straddling Tristan, as everything else becomes a blur.

Fingers tugging through hair.

Teeth scraping against skin.

Hands ripping off clothes.

Warm breath.

Soft moans.

He grips my hips and I grind against him, desperately craving a release. I feel him beneath me and his hardness is the perfect contrast to my wetness. Leaving our shirts on, we both readjust to slide my pants all the way off. Tristan pulls his down just enough to free his rock-solid cock before reaching in the console to tear open a foil packet. I don't have time to think about how many vehicular hookups he must have in order to warrant a car condom stash, because in one swift motion he's sheathed and pushing into me as his fingers dig roughly into my skin. I welcome the mix of pleasure and pain.

They say you always hurt the ones you love, and we've definitely had our fair share of both. Right now the awareness of the past is colliding with the uncertainty of the present and I can't tell if it's going to hurt or heal us.

My body feels like it's on fire as we move faster. With each thrust I feel another piece of me getting caught up in the storm that is Tristan Sharp. He brands me with each rough touch, his hands scouring every part of my body. His mouth finds my ear and he is hard and commanding as he grunts, "Can you feel me, Hazel? I want you to feel me everywhere."

As I get closer and closer to the edge of ecstasy, I dig my nails into his back, devouring the rawness of this moment. Just like the experience of getting high, having Tristan inside me makes me renounce every conscious thought. One minute I'm here, aware of every sound, touch, and sight, and the next I'm somewhere else outside my body, transcending all time, thought, and space.

Floating.

up, Up, UP.

Flying.

Euphoric.

Tingly. Senseless.

Numb.

I give myself over to the complete and utter ecstasy that occurs when you surrender every fiber of your being. My body is rendered paralyzed, but it's the kind of numb you experience as a result of feeling too much.

Tristan's release comes only seconds after mine and he murmurs "Fuck!" on a tortured groan as my muscles contract around him. A sheen of sweat covers both of our bodies and our breathing is hard and ragged. We fall silent as our heartbeats return to a normal pace.

I'm unaware of how many minutes pass before Tristan subtly clears his throat and I realize I'm still wrapped tightly around him. Startled by the tingling in my fingers and toes as I regain my senses, I ease off him and shift back over to the passenger seat. We each pull our pants back on without saying anything.

The clinking of Tristan's belt as he secures it around his waist is the loudest thing I've ever heard.

We sit in complete silence, fully clothed again in the dark. Things between us have never felt more awkward, and I'm wondering if he's completely regretting what just happened. I am searching for something, anything, to say to break the silence when a car barreling down the deserted road with its high beams on surprises us both.

Tristan glances in the rearview mirror and twists the key to turn the engine over. He sounds emotionless when he states, "I should get you home."

He doesn't look at me, instead focusing all his attention on driving to my house. I wasn't expecting to cuddle or share a cigarette or anything, but some type of acknowledgement that we just had explosive sex in his truck in the middle of the night might be nice.

Or maybe it was just explosive for me?

He pulls on to my street but stops the car before going up the driveway. All he says is, "We'll see each other around, OK?"

I nod, trying to feel nothing. *It was just sex, Hazel. Handle it.* "Yeah, see you around."

I get out of the truck and slam the door shut. As soon as I start walking up the drive I hear Tristan drive off. I should feel angry and used, and maybe part of me does, but I also don't remember a time I've felt more alive. Sure, it wasn't the first time I've had sex with Tristan Sharp, but it was the first time I was sober enough to feel something much deeper than just the physical part. If this is what it feels like to get to know Tristan Sharp again, I'm not sure what the hell I'm going to do about it.

STEP TWO: HOPE

We came to believe that a Power greater than ourselves could restore us to sanity.

CHAPTER

eleven

Eleven Years Ago

Tristan

"CAN YOU BELIEVE HOW CRAZY this shit is? Man, I fucking love high school," Logan yells over the loud music.

I look across the room and see two girls making out while a crowd surrounds them and cheers them on. I saw each chick do a keg stand about five minutes prior, so I'm sure that has something to do with their sudden mutual attraction.

House parties are pretty much a Friday night regular around here, and under normal circumstances I'd be just as thrilled as Logan to be witnessing this display. In fact I'm about to join him in the cheering, but when I catch a glimpse of Hazel with that asshole Dougie D, I can't focus on anything else. I look around the room for Ryan, hoping he's keeping tabs on his sister. I see him lounging in the kitchen with Johnny and they're both obviously trashed. I curse under my breath and put down my own beer to head in her direction.

I've been friends with Ryan and Hazel ever since Logan and I were placed in a foster home a few blocks from their house. When I was eight we were on the school playground eating lunch when I saw this douche named Bradley Nuberger try to steal an innocent little girl's sandwich. It wasn't that I was particularly chivalrous, but the kid had spent the morning shooting spitballs at my head so I was looking for a chance to deck him. Just as I got ready to kick him in the shins, this spunky little girl pulled her arm back and knocked his front tooth out. Then she cried on my shoulder because she felt bad.

I'm not sure if that was the exact moment I fell in love with Hazel Blake, but it sure was the moment I felt this instinctive duty to protect her. Sure she was tough on the outside, but she still needed someone to comfort her.

And I liked feeling needed.

As we grew up, Logan and I fell into a good rhythm with Ryan and his best friend, Lucas, and the four of us became tight. Once puberty hit I found myself drawn to Hazel's soft curves and beautiful face, but since she's Ryan's little sister I've tried to keep my horny hands to myself. Recently I've noticed her falling in with a bad crowd—the kind of people known for doing and dealing drugs. It might not be any of my business, but I can't sit back and watch Hazel get messed up in that shit. It's not the first time I've seen her with this douche Dougie, but I certainly want it to be the last.

I walk up beside her, shoving my hands casually in my pockets. "Hey."

She smiles when she sees me. "Hey, yourself."

A tipsy girl stumbles near us, and I use the opportunity to grab Hazel's hips and move her a few steps to the right, away from Dougie.

"What's up? I haven't seen you around lately." I try to keep the conversation casual, stalling as I think of how to get her out of here.

She shrugs. "Not much. You know, just hanging out." She looks back at Dougie, who is talking in hushed tones to someone else. I catch what I perceive as a hint of anxiety in Hazel's eyes, so I figure now is my chance.

"Hey, you wanna get out of here for a bit?"

Almost immediately she responds, "Sure."

I grab her hand and pull her through the crowded party. We go outside and get in my car, a beat-up Chevy that Logan and I bought after saving every penny we made for a year.

I start driving and only a few miles later we pull down a dirt road that leads to a small wooded clearing. It's practically hidden if you don't know about it, but I accidentally discovered the path a few months ago when my foster mother pissed me off. Ever since, I've been coming here when I need someplace to get away. By the way lights from the town shine in the distance and the stars twinkle above, it feels like you're in the middle of some sort of galaxy—a private universe where time moves at its own pace and everything is art.

I pull the car under a set of trees off to the left, and Hazel looks around in fascination as she gets out.

"What is this place?" she asks.

I pop the trunk and grab an old blanket. "A secret."

She tilts her head up to the sky and wraps her arms around herself.

I spread the blanket out on the ground and sit down.

I try not to let it get to me that I can smell Hazel's hair as she settles down next to me.

"I like it here."

"I like it, too."

"Tell me something about yourself."

"Like what?"

"I don't know. Since this is a secret place, why not tell me a secret about yourself?"

I grunt. "I hate mushrooms. They creep me out."

"For real?" Hazel laughs. I think it's my favorite sound.

"Yup. They're spongy and weird and I can't stand them." I nod at her. "Your turn."

She thinks about it for a second. "Someday I want to live in a house with a purple door."

Not what I was expecting. "How come?" I genuinely want to know.

She lifts her shoulder, then lets it drop. "Because I want to. And it's just a bonus that it would piss off my mother. She'd be horrified." She laughs again. Yup, definitely my favorite sound.

"Fair enough."

"So is this where you lure girls to try and seduce them?" She changes the subject.

I lean back on my hands and smirk. "Maybe. Would you like to be seduced?"

She shrugs, trying to conceal her own smile. "Maybe. Although you'd actually be the first to try."

I raise an eyebrow. "Come on, I don't believe that." The thought of Hazel with anybody else suddenly makes me angry.

"I guess that's another secret you know about me now."

"Seriously?"

She blushes. "I'm sure you must think that's super lame."

"Why would I think that?"

"Because I see the way girls throw themselves at you."

"So?"

"So I'm sure you'd rather be out having fun with one of them than sitting here with me talking about how I haven't even had my first kiss yet."

"I'm the one who asked you here, remember?"

She smiles before looking out at the lights shining in the distance. "True."

I stare at her. I can't help myself. She's nothing I expected, yet everything I want.

She notices I'm staring.

She asks in a soft voice, "Why do you look at me like that?"

"Like what?"

"Like you see me."

"Because I do."

A pause.

"We should probably get back to the party." She says this, but doesn't move.

I keep my eyes locked with hers.

"Yeah, we probably should." I don't move either.

Another pause.

"Hazel," I say, exhaling a sharp breath.

"Yeah," she says, inhaling a sharp breath.

"Want to know another secret?"

I lean forward.

She nods.

In one quick, fluid motion I grab her neck, pulling it so close my lips can taste hers.

My tongue slips past her teeth, and she makes the most arousing noise in the back of her throat that reverberates through her entire body.

With my eyes closed I get to see her in a whole new way.

Her skin is soft and warm.

She smells like flowers.

Our mouths fit perfectly together.

For thirty whole seconds nothing has ever felt more right.

I pull back because I need to look at her again. Her green eyes sparkle back.

"That was my first kiss, too."

She smiles before biting her lip.

Turns out we would be each other's firsts in ways that went way past kissing.

STEP THREE: FAITH

We made a decision to turn our will and our lives over to the care of God as we understood Him.

CHAPTER

twelve

Tristan

REMEMBER WHEN I THOUGHT SCREWING Hazel Blake would get her out of my system?

Turns out that was a huge crock of shit.

It's been three days since we fucked in my truck and I'm no closer to forgetting her than I was before our roadside quickie. Hopefully some exercise will help clear my head.

I'm shooting a few quick hoops with Logan and Lucas for our usual Friday, post-work game at the park. The basketball court is off to the side of a large, grassy field and is surrounded by picnic tables. A few yards away are a small swing set and slide. It's a cool, crisp evening, and despite the ominous dark clouds in the sky, we figured we could at least get a quick game in.

Ryan used to join us, too, but ever since he knocked up Kelley we haven't seen much of him. Probably for the best, especially after what happened at the baby shower.

I shuffle my feet and move to steal the basketball before going in for a layup. *Swish.*

"Jesus, Luc, where were you on that one?" Logan chokes,

trying to catch his breath.

Before he can respond I interject with "Ever since he got hitched he's lost his edge. Must be too tired from picking out china patterns or doing couple's yoga or whatever the fuck it is married people do." I toss the ball back to Lucas.

"You're just jealous, man. Unlike you, I no longer have to troll bars in order to get laid. Monogamy has its perks. You might want to try it sometime."

I roll my eyes. I'd never admit I'm secretly happy for the guy. If anyone deserves a good relationship it's Lucas. He's probably one of the most loyal, honest people I know. But he doesn't need that shit going to his head, so instead I snicker. "You know who always tries to convince you fucking one person for the rest of your life is actually a good thing? Resentful married guys who realize they're the ones who will only get to fuck one person for the rest of their lives."

Both Lucas and Logan laugh before moving to the side of the court to get a drink of water. I follow suit, grabbing my phone from my duffle bag to check my text messages. I have a few updates from CJ about the Collins Street house and a note about a shipment of lumber I ordered, but it's the last message that makes me tense.

HAZEL: Hey. I think we should talk . . . come over tonight?

Fuck. This can't be good.

I debate not answering, but I know that would only delay shit. Better to man up and get this over with.

ME: I'll be there in an hour.

I throw my phone back in my bag and sling it over my shoulder.

"Where you off to, bro? I thought we were going to Chaser's

for a drink." Logan looks confused.

I shake my head. "Something came up. Rain check?"

"Fine, but remember we have that party for DSGN tomorrow night."

"I thought you guys got rid of them ages ago." I swear I can't keep up with Logan and Lucas' venture capital firm. How that world works seems like a bunch of bullshit, if you ask me. I prefer to get my hands dirty with some good old-fashioned manual labor, but to each his own. I guess they know what they're doing. And I'm certainly not one to turn down a free invite.

"Technically we made our investment back so they bought us out, but we keep in touch. Ever since they signed with Parker & Peterman Industries and went public last year their stock has skyrocketed. They have more money than they know what to do with." He zips up his sweatshirt and smiles. "Hey, it's free booze and babes."

"Then I'm there."

I say goodbye to the guys and head to my truck. I have just enough time to go home and shower before going to Hazel's. Time to figure our shit out so I can get back to my life.

CHAPTER
thirteen

Hazel

I SEE THE FLASH OF Tristan's headlights as he pulls up to the pool house right at eight. I'm actually kind of surprised he didn't blow me off.

After the other night, once my lust-induced stupor wore off, I realized that as much as I might always have feelings for Tristan, he probably will never feel the same about me . . . and I can't say I blame him. I may be clean now, but that doesn't mean my destructive tendencies have magically disappeared. Every single day it's a struggle to make the right choices. I live with a constant fear of fucking things up again, and I think I've hurt Tristan enough for one lifetime already. I have no business trying to start up a serious relationship with him, nor do I want to risk hurting him. All I want is a friend, and Tristan always understood me better than anyone.

But there is also no denying that we definitely share a mutual physical attraction, so is it really so wrong to indulge in that, if we both agree it's just sex? I'm not sure I can fully explain the feeling I got having Tristan consume every part of me in his truck the other night, but it's something I'd do anything to experience again. All we need to do is talk and get everything out in the open. Then we can start over.

Above the mellow beat of the music I have playing throughout the apartment I hear him knock. I smooth my hair and my dress and open the door, smiling. "Hey, I'm glad you came."

A crack of thunder booms in the distance.

He moves past me and before I can even pretend to make small talk he asks, "What do you want to talk about?"

I close the door, lean against it, and take one big, deep breath to settle my nerves. "I want to know why you really wanted to fuck me the other night," I blurt. "You went from barely talking on the way to the baby shower to practically stalking me at three in the morning. Was it just some type of revenge? A sick way to get back at me for . . . for what I did?" My stomach rolls at the thought, not because I'd blame him, but because I know I'd deserve it. I mean look at me; I can barely admit out loud that I broke his heart in the most cruel, selfish way possible.

Tristan grins. "And what if it was?" Another loud roar of thunder cuts through the air, this time sounding closer.

My heart drops. "I get it, T, you're mad at me. Hell, I'm mad at me, too. I did a lot of stuff I wish I could take back and I'm just trying to get past it all. But I really didn't call you to stir shit up. I hoped maybe enough time had passed that we could just see where things go and maybe be friends again." My voice trails off as I realize how inadequate that sounds.

"And why the hell do you want to be friends with me?" Tristan spits roughly. His anger is more than justified, but it still hurts.

I admit truthfully, "Because you were my best friend, Tristan. And I fucked it up. And maybe it's selfish of me, but you were the only person who ever seemed to care about me. I don't have anybody else."

He stands his ground, staring at me. "I can't save you, Hazel. I'm not that guy. I never was. Now I prefer to keep my shit to myself and fuck for the fun of it. I don't do commitment and I like to keep my options open. I'm not interested in or capable of anything more."

My lungs constrict at his brutal honesty, but I understand. "Then it's a good thing I'm not looking for more," I reply, forcing myself to look at his face, even though I can't make direct eye contact. "I'm not exactly in a position to get involved with anyone, not in any serious way. I've spent my entire life trying to escape who I was and now I just want a chance to be free . . . to live in the moment and figure the rest out as I go."

"What are you saying, Hazel?" His voice is low and gravelly. Rain starts to pelt the roof and windows.

I take a slow step closer, then another, then another until I'm right in front of him. The sexy, low beat of the music, mixed with the rhythm of the pouring rain, emphasizes every stride. "I'm saying you were right about one thing." I flick my eyes down his body. "There is one part of our relationship that we've always been good at." I finally gain the courage to look into his eyes, even though I'm terrified he really wants nothing to do with me anymore. Thankfully I see lust, mixed with a hint of amusement.

"And you're cool with just being fuck buddies?"

The harshness of hearing the words out loud makes me cringe, but what did I really expect?

I suddenly want to tell him the truth . . . that I want so much more with him; that I'm so sorry I ever hurt him and that I would never let it happen again. I've spent so much of my life hiding things that part of me wants a chance to break free from all the secrets.

But my mother's voice rings in my head: *Just remember, a*

leopard doesn't change its spots.

After the way I treated Tristan, he has every right to not trust me. I don't even know if I can trust myself. But there is something deep in my gut that screams at me to hold onto the only piece of us that might work, even if it's just physical, so I simply nod in agreement before meeting his lips in a hard, hungry kiss.

I grip his shoulders as his hands find my hips. He lets me taste him for one delicious minute before pulling back. "You know I hate you," he says. Lightning flashes brightly, lighting up his face long enough for me to see the fire in his eyes.

I push my lips back against his and whisper, "You can hate me, as long as you're inside me."

The real truth is that I need Tristan like I need air, and right now I'm willing to do anything to be able to breathe.

As we kiss he walks backward, leading me to the couch, his strong arms wrapped tightly around my waist. I resist his hold and push his chest roughly so he falls back on the cushioned seat. I climb on his lap to straddle him, my dress rising up my thighs.

I rush to pull his shirt over his head, needing the heat of his skin on mine. As my hands travel down his toned arms they skim over a bold tattoo on his left bicep, and patches of smooth and jagged skin on his right. I pause when I feel the tender skin, remembering that I used to trace these same scars so many years ago. I never asked what happened but I know it has something to do with his mother. The sadness I feel makes me shudder. There is still so much about this man I don't know.

The scrape of Tristan's teeth on my neck as he arches me back makes me cry out wildly, my voice mingling with the sound of thunder. His callused hands dig sharply into my ribs and I drag my fingers through his hair, grabbing the ends. It's like all the pain from our entire lives comes storming to the surface and the only way we know how to deal with it is to take it out on each other.

I push.

He pushes harder.

He moans.

I moan louder.

But every ounce of physical pain we deliver is matched by an equal amount of faith. Faith that this will somehow fix us.

He yanks my dress over my head before tearing my underwear from my body. He looks like he's ready to devour me whole.

God, I'll let him.

He lifts us off the couch and flattens my back on the smooth wooden coffee table. Within seconds he lowers his pants, just enough to free his thick, hard cock. He pulls a foil packet from his pocket, tears it open with his teeth, and rolls it down his length.

I don't even have time to fully process this before I feel his weight on me and he's thrusting inside my wet and ready core. I dig my nails into his back, causing him to growl as he pounds into me faster. It only takes a few seconds before I'm careening over the edge, crying out, but still he refuses to slow down.

"You like feeling me inside you, Hazel?" Tristan grits from behind clenched teeth. "You like it when I make you scream?"

I mumble something that sounds like "Mmmmfuckyyyeesssss," as I rake my right hand up his back to his short, dark hair. I let my fingers massage gently before tugging roughly.

His head falls back and I use the opportunity to gain leverage. Still grabbing his hair with my right hand, I use my left to shove his chest so we fall back on the couch. His mouth finds my breast as I settle my knees on either side of him, his tongue swirling around my nipple before gently biting it.

He drives his dick back up inside me and I press my pelvis down to create more friction. I wrap my arms around his neck, holding him tightly to my chest as I move my hips and feel every inch of him fill me to the point of breaking.

It's painful in the most beautiful way.

For the next hour we fuck hard and we fuck fast and we fuck all over my apartment until neither of us has any fight left.

Yes, Tristan Sharp can hate me, but I'm going to make sure he loves every second of it.

CHAPTER

fourteen

Tristan

AFTER I REGAIN FEELING IN my body, I look over to Hazel. By the way her breathing has slowed to a steady pace, I know she's fallen asleep. She's lying on the bed face down, her back bare with the sheets draped over her lower half. Her hair is splayed across the pillow. Tattoos litter her shoulders, back, and upper arms.

For someone who looks so tough, she sure seems vulnerable when she's naked.

When we're together it's almost like nothing's changed between us, but there's also something different about her—something sad. It makes me feel like an asshole, even though *she's* the one who seduced *me* tonight. Not that I was about to complain. Sure, being around her tends to mess with my head, but since we made it crystal clear that what we're doing is just fucking, at least it's honest. Hell, maybe it will even help relieve some of my pent-up anger toward her. If Hazel Blake wants to use me for sex, I'm more than willing to do the same.

I pull on my pants and get up to take a leak. I find a small bathroom connected to the bedroom and take care of business. As I'm washing up I notice a shampoo bottle on the edge of the tub. I pick it up and look at the label: citrus mint. I inhale a deep whiff and yup, that's definitely Hazel. *Mint*. Go figure.

I walk back out to the bedroom and in the light coming from the bathroom I finally notice the room. I was a little preoccupied throwing Hazel down and screwing her senseless when I first came in.

The queen bed, where Hazel is still out cold, is in the far corner. My attention is drawn to the white walls, where a bunch of black-and-white photographs are taped up in some type of collage. Hazel took up photography after high school, but it's just one of the many reminders of a past I wish I could forget.

My curiosity gets the better of me, though, so I lean in closer. I recognize a few of the pictures from when Hazel was younger. Some of her as a little girl, some of her and Ryan, and even a few of us from high school. I study each photo and thank fuck there are none of Dougie. If there were, I'd probably put my fist through the wall.

Amidst the older snapshots are a bunch of newer photos that all have a similar, artistic style to them. One is of a rose, and at first glance it seems to be a simple flower, but when you look closer you can see the petals' edges are torn and withered. Another is a close-up of a sidewalk with weeds and roots growing up through the cracks. There is also a series of self-portraits, where Hazel seems to be holding the camera herself, trying out different angles that capture only a small piece of her at a time. An eye, her hand, a shoulder. I don't know much about art or photography, but it's the imperfection of each image that makes them interesting. They're real and unfiltered, which is unusual since most people I know are more interested in pretending they're perfect.

Something about seeing these makes me feel weird. Privileged, almost. Like I'm getting some secret glimpse into the real Hazel. I shake the feeling off, remembering there's no point in wanting or trying to get to know her. I did that once before, only to have it thrown in my face. We come from different worlds and want different things, and no matter what she does or says, that won't change. I never knew the real Hazel, nor do I have any interest in once again making the mistake of thinking I do. I just need to treat her like I would any other girl I'm fucking—keep things fun and friendly—and walk away when I'm finished. No opening up, no expectations, and certainly no commitment. Done deal.

I see a Polaroid camera sitting on the desk and pick it up. I look at Hazel, whose body is cast in the glow from the bathroom light. She looks so peaceful and so innocent that I lift the camera to my eye, focus on her face, and push the button. A second later a square of film pops out the bottom.

I place the camera back on the desk and grab a pen, scribble a quick note across the bottom of the photo and place it on the pillow beside Hazel. Then I grab the rest of my clothes and let myself out.

You're beautiful after we "talk." Call me if you want to do it again sometime.

THE NEXT NIGHT I FIND myself standing next to Logan at the DSGN party, but for the first time ever I have no real interest in being here. I've instead been more interested in checking my phone constantly, hoping like some sort of deprived sex junkie that my next "talk" with Hazel will be sooner rather than later. Hey, if she's offering me only her body, without any of the other bullshit relationship stuff, I'd be an idiot not to accept. I may not want to be friends, but I sure could get used to the fucking part. And once I've had my fill I can forget her for good.

I look up and see Lucas arrive.

I expect to see Kinsley with him. What I don't expect is to see Kinsley *and* Hazel.

"What's up?" Lucas greets Logan and me while I try to keep my excitement in my pants.

"Didn't know you were coming, Zee." Logan smiles at Hazel. She's looking particularly fuckable in a tight black dress and matching high heels.

"Kinsley invited me this afternoon, so I figured why not come and see what all the fuss is about." Her eyes dart to me before settling back on my brother. "I hope that's OK."

Kinsley pipes up, "Since Kelley's been busy growing that tiny human of hers I've missed having a partner in crime. I needed somebody to help deal with you three." She laughs, looking hot in a yellow strapless dress, with her hair pulled back. Lucas is a lucky man, that's for sure.

Yes, think about Kinsley. Think about anything other than how much you want to be buried inside Hazel again.

I clear my throat, pulling myself together. "Correct me if I'm wrong, Kins, but wasn't it the last DSGN party where we first met?" I raise my eyebrows and pat Lucas on the shoulder. "If it wasn't for this over-possessive Neanderthal maybe you'd be here on my arm instead of his." Everyone laughs, but by the way Lucas edges closer to Kinsley and wraps his arm around her waist, I know the thought rattles him. You'd think messing with him would get old, but it really doesn't.

"We better go find Eric," Lucas says to Logan, talking about the CEO of DSGN.

"Oh I'd love to say hi, too," Kinsley adds. She turns to Hazel, "Will you be OK by yourself for a little bit?" To me she says, "I'm sure Tristan will keep you company until I get back."

"I think we'll manage to find a way to occupy ourselves." I resist the urge to fist pump and smile as innocently as possible while the rest of the group leaves.

As soon as they are out of earshot Hazel glares at me. "What the hell are you doing? You want everyone to know we're . . . that we . . ."

She struggles to find the words, and I have to admit I find it adorably amusing. I give her another few seconds to flounder before offering, "Fucked?"

She points at me with the small black purse she's gripping. "Exactly."

"Listen, do you really think I want to chance Ryan finding out about us by telling everyone? Dude already has it out for me."

Hazel smiles mischievously. "So you think there is some kind of *us*?"

"An *us* that fucks occasionally." I grin.

"Right. So we're in agreement to keep this quiet?"

"Agreed."

"Should we shake on it or something?" Hazel laughs.

"I have a better idea."

I grab Hazel's hand and pull her through the crowded room. We head out of the main space and find a secluded spot at the end of the hall that's hidden behind the curtains separating the caterer's workspace. It's a tight, narrow spot nestled between the curtain and a wall, but it will get the job done.

As soon as we're out of sight I grab Hazel by the neck, kissing her roughly while simultaneously pushing her against the wall. She moans into my mouth, dropping her purse to the floor. It's been less than 24 hours since I've touched her, but man, I'm like a dog with a friggin' bone.

She pulls her face back and her fingers move to the small

buttons on my white shirt. She takes her time undoing each one, clearly trying to torture me.

When she's finally finished I reach for the hem of her dress and pull it up just past her hips before helping her as she struggles with the zipper on my pants. She's trying to play it cool, but I can tell she's worked up. Maybe even more than I am. Suddenly I want her to beg for me.

I grab her hands and hold them above her head against the wall. I move my mouth close to hers but don't let our lips touch. She tries to extend her lower half to rub against mine. I remain just close enough that she can feel my dominance, but refuse to give her what she craves.

I look into her eyes, silently challenging us both. It's an unspoken test to see who will give in first. She holds my stare for a few moments before squeezing her eyes shut and throwing her head back in defeat.

I win.

I can't help but get a thrill out of how much this girl wants me. Call me a vindictive prick, but after spending time feeling worthless and empty when she rejected me all those years ago, hearing her beg for me on a pleasured moan over and over is like the sickest form of revenge. Hazel Blake is the kind of girl that will kiss you until it hurts and I'll be damned if I let her have the chance.

Not sure how long I can withstand my own torment, with expert efficiency I grab a condom from my pocket and roll it on. I grab her ass and grind her lower back into the wall for support. I position myself at her entrance, rubbing the head of my dick against her clit. Her breath hitches as I tease us both. I slip the tip of my dick inside the tight opening of her pussy, then pull out. She makes a frustrated sound in the back of her throat.

I push back in a little deeper, then retreat. More frustrated sounds.

Her eyes lock on mine and I hold my throbbing cock right up against her. We stand there for a beat, challenging each other once again, before I drive into her with such a satisfying thrust that we both moan in relief.

Hazel's hands grip my shoulders like a vice as I pound into her, no longer holding back. Each stroke gets faster and goes deeper. I sure hope the caterers don't decide now is a good time to clean up, because I'm not stopping even if they do.

Her right leg wraps around my back and I can feel the blunt spike of her heel digging into my flesh. Her left leg remains on the floor and she uses it as leverage to buck her hips wildly against mine, meeting each of my thrusts with her own. I can't tell who is in control. At this exact moment I'm not sure I even care.

I allow my mouth to explore her neck, needing to taste some part of her skin. She stifles another moan and I know she's getting close. I slow my pace just enough to really draw out her undoing. I want her to come apart, and I want her to know it's because of *me*.

She buries her face in my shoulder and I feel her teeth leave marks as she gives herself over to me completely.

Only when I know she's finished riding the satisfying wave of ecstasy do I allow myself to follow, spasming with the intensity of feeling her tight wetness pulse around me. She opens her eyes and looks into mine, gently biting her lip.

I reach into my pocket for a handkerchief to clean myself up. I pull up my pants and Hazel pulls her dress down. She looks tousled and spent in the most satisfying way possible, and the sick part of me once again revels in the fact that I have that effect on her. She certainly fucks with my head, so it's only fair I return the favor.

I kneel down to pick up her purse with one hand, dragging

the fingers of the other slowly up her leg. She sucks in a breath as I stop right between her thighs, then hand her purse over. "You head back in and I'll follow in a minute."

She takes her purse in one hand and smoothes her hair with the other. Before she leaves she turns back and says, "Remember, we can't tell anyone about this."

"Some of the best moments are the ones you can't tell anyone about." I wink and she blushes in the sexiest, most mischievous way before leaving.

When I'm alone, suddenly winning doesn't seem nearly as gratifying. As much as I might affect Hazel, she still does the same goddamn thing to me. No matter how much I try to make her suffer, she serves it right back.

I hate that. But apparently, not enough to stop.

I rest my head back against the wall. As I button up my shirt I try to figure out how the hell I got myself into this situation. I can only pray I know what the fuck I'm doing.

CHAPTER

fifteen

Eleven years ago

Hazel

"COME ON, HAZEL, JUST TRY it. I promise it makes everything better. You'll like it."

I stare at the rolled-up bill in Dougie's outstretched hand before reaching out to accept it.

I lower my head to look at the white powder lined up on the mirror. I can see my eyes reflected back above it. I look scared. I feel scared.

I also feel sad and angry and hurt and invisible and lost, and I don't want to anymore. I don't want to feel anything. It's too much. I can't breathe.

I bring the paper tube to my nose, lean over, and inhale deeply.

My nose burns, along with the back of my throat, so I squeeze my eyes shut. I hear Dougie say it will get better, so I clench my teeth and wait.

He's right. The burning doesn't last.

I wait some more.

The bliss that overtakes me isn't instantaneous, but then, all of a *sudden, I come alive.*

I'm floating. Floating so high I'm flying.

I'm tingly. I'm senseless. I'm numb.

No more anxiety, no more fear, no more sadness.

No more bad feelings, period. Just a sense of purpose. A feeling that I'm now complete.

I'm somebody, now. Somebody you can see.

And this is what makes me, me.

CHAPTER

sixteen

Hazel

MUSIC FILLS MY HEAD AS I get off the bus in the center of town. It's been five days since the DSGN party, and while Tristan and I have texted a little (yes, mostly dirty stuff), we haven't been able to . . . *hang out*. I know it's best for me to keep busy, which is why I plan to look for a second job.

But I still need to repay Tristan, both for the ride to the baby shower and for driving me home from the diner. So today I thought I'd surprise him before searching for employment.

And OK, it's really just a shameless ploy to see him.

I walk up to the small construction office, which is nestled between a realtor's office and a print shop, and breathe a quick sigh of relief that it's still in the same spot. I pull my earbuds from my ears and tuck them into my bag. Holding a paper bag filled with homemade sandwiches in one hand and running my fingers through my hair with the other, I knock and hear, "Come in.".

Mr. Turner is sitting behind a big wooden desk. He looks exactly the same as I remember. As he looks up and takes off his glasses I worry he won't recognize me, but after only a second, recognition passes over his features.

"Hazel Blake?"

I nod and he stands up to greet me with a warm smile.

"I was afraid you wouldn't remember me." I chuckle nervously.

"How could I ever forget the girl who used to hang around all the time? Heck, you were around so much I thought I would have to start paying you."

I smile at the memories of waiting for Tristan to get off work on nights and weekends. We'd sometimes grab a bite to eat, or just go somewhere and talk, but no matter what we did it always felt . . . perfect.

Mr. Turner continues, "What in the world brings you around this old place?"

"I was wondering if you could tell me where Tristan is working today. I brought him some lunch." I hold up the paper bag as evidence of my claim.

Mr. Turner grins widely. "I should have guessed you'd be here to see him and not me. I didn't realize you guys were together again."

I wave my hands, causing the lunch bag to crinkle loudly. "Oh no, it's not like that. We're just friends."

Mr. Turner studies me for a solid five seconds. "Of course. My mistake." He sits back in his chair, puts his glasses on, and starts shuffling some papers on his desk. "I think he was planning on helping over on Collins Street today. Just a few blocks that way." He looks up from the papers and points out the right side of the front picture window.

"Thanks so much." I start to leave, then turn back. I always liked Mr. Turner, and I suddenly feel the need to express my fondness. "You know, I was really happy to hear Tristan is still working here. I know he always looked up to you and this job means a lot to him."

"That boy was my best worker from the very first day he started. He had an attitude and a mouth on him, but he always worked hard. Not much has changed. Well, except for the fact *he* now has to sign *my* paychecks." He chuckles.

Tristan signs paychecks? "What do you mean? Did he get a promotion or something?"

"I'd say becoming owner of the company would count as one hell of a promotion." He quirks an eyebrow. "He didn't mention it?"

I shake my head, trying to keep the confusion and hurt from showing on my face.

Mr. Turner apparently takes pity on me. "Last year I decided this job was becoming a little too much for me to handle. When Tristan found out I was looking for a buyer, he made an offer. I knew there was no one I'd trust more. And ever since, he's been doing one hell of a job. I stay on part-time, mostly doing office work here, but to be honest I feel sort of useless with how well he has things handled."

I'm proud of Tristan for being so successful, but I'm also pissed he didn't want to share this information with me. I guess we're really not friends anymore.

I swallow the pang of irritation. "That's really great." I motion to the door. "Well, I should get going and deliver the boss his lunch." I smile. "It was good to see you, Mr. Turner."

"You, too, Hazel. Feel free to stop by any time."

I nod appreciatively and make for the door.

I spend the short walk to the construction site feeling more and more angry at Tristan, ready to give him a piece of my mind. But as soon as I see him, I freeze.

He's wearing a pair of work boots, ripped jeans and a white

tank top, all smudged with dirt. He is standing next to a small group of teenage boys and appears to be showing them how to secure a beam properly. One boy tries to mimic what Tristan just demonstrated, but the beam slides out of his grasp. Tristan catches it easily, and smiles encouragement as he lets the boy try again. This time the kid does it successfully, and all the boys look at Tristan with trust and admiration. He pats the boy on his shoulder, letting him take over. Tristan then hoists a stack of wooden boards over his well-muscled shoulder, which is covered with a glistening sheen of sweat.

He looks solid and strong and I find myself short of breath. Sure he looks hot as hell, but it's something else that makes my knees weak. The determination and pride that emanates from his every pore is something I never noticed before. I find myself marveling that Charter Hill is lucky to have someone so strong and committed to look after things. Mr. Turner was right to trust him.

Tristan walks toward me and I can barely remember my own name, let alone why I should be mad. He stops a few feet away to drop the boards on the ground, and I'm pretty sure I literally lick my lips as I check out the way his ass looks when he bends over.

"Hey, what are you doing here? . . . Hazel?"

I snap my eyes up to his, embarrassed that he just caught me staring. "I, uh . . ." I go to wipe my forehead, realizing the paper bag's still gripped in my now-sweaty palm, and silently curse myself for getting so tongue tied when I'm around this guy. All I can come up with is "Food?" as I hold up the bag.

Tristan chuckles and steps forward to take the bag. He leans close to my ear and whispers, "Don't worry, I don't mind if you look. As long as you promise to touch later." He pulls back and winks in his usual damn cocky way, which thankfully is all it takes to break my trance.

"Eh, the view's not that great, OK? Besides, I have plans tonight, so it looks like you'll have to sleep alone." Plans I'd gladly change if he really wants me to. I don't need to look for a second job that badly, right?

He wiggles his eyebrows. "Sleeping alone is a waste of my bedroom talents. You should know that by now."

I want to argue just to put him in his place, but he's not wrong . . .

I settle for crossing my arms and shaking my head.

"I'm just teasing you, Hazel, relax. I'm busy tonight anyway."

"Really?" I try to keep the disappointment out of my voice. "Anything fun?" I ask, a little too pointedly.

Tristan shrugs and peeks into the paper bag. He pulls out the sandwich and examines it.

"It's peanut butter and jelly. I remember we used to eat them when we were younger." I try not to frown. "I wasn't sure what you like these days."

He looks at me strangely. A grown man like Tristan probably doesn't eat PB&Js anymore.

Before he can say anything, someone calls his name from across the lot. He looks relieved and hooks his thumb backward saying, "I should probably get back."

"Of course. I didn't mean to keep you." As I turn to leave, I hear him say my name and glance back to see him holding up the sandwich.

"Thanks," he says. "I'll text you later, OK?"

I nod and smile back, comforted by the hope of making plans with him again soon.

I HEAD INTO A PLACE called Chaser's around seven o'clock.

I heard they were looking for a new waitress and want to check it out. Working in a bar might not seem like the best place for a recovering addict, but, if I get the job, I'm determined to prove to myself I can handle it. Life is full of temptation and I don't want to hide from it.

I check to make sure my resume is still in my bag, even though I'm praying they don't actually want to see it. Even after bumping up the font a few sizes and adding plenty of spacing to the lines, it's more than obvious I don't have much experience.

As I walk up to the bar I notice Logan sitting at the far end nursing a beer, alone. I slide onto the stool next to him. "You know it's bad luck to drink alone."

Logan looks surprised, but seems genuinely happy to see me. "I've always liked to push my luck, haven't I?" He smiles, his adorable dimples on full display. "Good thing you're here to save me from myself. Can I buy you a drink?"

While Logan and Tristan aren't identical twins, they certainly share many of the same features: same brown eyes and same square jaw, but where Tristan's hair is dark, Logan's is blond, and Logan's cheeks are dotted with the most adorable set of dimples. Tristan and I had an instant, deep bond right from the beginning, but Logan and I became friends when we were younger, too, just in a different way. He was like another big brother to me, always teasing me and giving me a hard time, along with Ryan and Lucas.

Logan swallows down the last of his drink. His eyes appear glassy, making me think he's already had quite a few.

"Thanks, but I'm good. You know, recovering drug addict and all that. Drinking is considered a gateway."

"Right. Sorry." He grips the empty bottle in his hands. "How is all that?"

"I'm fine, really." I wave him off, not wanting to get into it.

"Is Tristan here?" I look around, getting a little too excited at the idea that this is what Tristan meant by having plans. If I run into him by accident I can't come across as desperate or stalkerish, right?

"Nah, I'm flying solo tonight. It's Thursday, which means my brother is otherwise occupied."

"Occupied?" My heart sinks.

"Every Thursday, Tristan always has plans. I'm pretty sure he has a standing date, if you catch my drift." Logan chuckles and motions to the bartender for another beer.

My stomach churns at the thought of Tristan with another woman. I know it shouldn't, but it does. I bet it's that giggly bitch. Maybe when he said she isn't exactly his girlfriend he meant she's really just his Thursday night fuck buddy. "He's just full of surprises, isn't he?" I mutter under my breath.

"Hmm?"

I shake my head. "Nothing. Can I ask you something?"

"Shoot."

The bartender puts a new bottle of Sam Adams in front of Logan before looking at me. I shake my head and wave to say I'm all set, then turn back to Logan. "Did you know Tristan owns Charter Hill now?"

He gives me a look that indicates he has no idea why I'd be asking. "Of course. Why, what's the big deal?"

"I'm just curious as to why he wouldn't mention it to me. Seems like a pretty basic detail." I shrug, trying to appear indifferent, but I think a part of me hoped he was keeping it a secret from everyone so I wouldn't have to feel so excluded.

"Should he have mentioned it to you? No offense, Zee, but I didn't think you two were still close. Unless I'm wrong . . . ?" Logan appears both confused and amused.

Shit. My stupid obsession with wanting to know more about

Tristan's life is going to get us busted. "Not really. I mean, other than when he gave me a ride to the baby shower. We caught up a little then, but he really didn't seem to want to share much about himself."

"Well you did fuck him up pretty good. At least, I'm assuming you did. Tristan never wants to talk about you, so I know something is up. Care to enlighten me, little Zee?"

Logan smiles mischievously and I look away. No matter how much I wish I could take back everything I did to Tristan, I'm constantly reminded how badly I screwed this all up. "I . . . we . . . uhh . . ." I struggle, trying to find the words, before settling with a truthful, "It's complicated." I hate that I'm still too embarrassed to talk about what happened.

He shrugs, giving me the same brush-off Tristan usually does. "Well, sometimes guys just don't want to share every last detail of their lives. It's not a big deal."

I study Logan's face, seeing now more than ever the resemblance to his brother. "You two are so alike, you know that? So nonchalant about everything. You don't seem to have a care in the world. I'm jealous, because I can't ever get my mind to shut up."

"Well we *are* twins." He flashes his signature dimpled smile. "But can I tell you a secret?" He leans in, close enough that I can smell the liquor on his breath, and whispers, "It's all bullshit." He returns to a normal volume. "Sure, we joke and have a good time, but it's only to cover the fact that the rest of our lives are pretty empty. People expect us to party and get laid—which we do because, well, having something is better than nothing, but this sleeping around bullshit is getting old quick. We're not getting any younger and I don't know about T, but I'm sure as shit over playing all the games. If I found the right girl, I know I'd be ready to settle down."

By the way some of his words slur a little, I can tell for sure Logan is tipsy at this point, but something about the look on his face indicates there's a painful truth about what he says. And it makes me feel sad.

I know what it's like to have people judge you based on how you look and act, without ever really knowing the whole story. I realize I've done this myself, assuming things about Tristan without ever having the courage to ask him straight out. I guess I've been afraid the truth would somehow hurt more than not knowing.

I know something has to change between us, because as much as I don't want to lose the physical stuff Tristan and I share, I also need him to give me something more. I'm not asking for an exclusive relationship, but I at least need him to be able to talk to me as a friend if we're going to continue to be around each other.

I just hope I'm ready to hear what he has to say.

CHAPTER
seventeen

Hazel

I GET OFF THE BUS at 9:45pm and check my phone for the bajillionth time since last night. After I made sure Logan got a cab home and left my resume with the bartender at Chaser's, I sat up half the night, hoping Tristan might still text me after his . . . *date*.

The thought continues to make my stomach twist, but not as much as the fact that I haven't heard from him.

A wave of disappointment washes over me when there are still no message notifications on my screen, so I shove it back in my bag along with my earbuds and open the door to the diner. Nan is already inside. We occasionally work the same shift on Friday nights, which tend to be busy, and the place is already crowded. While I'm not exactly in a chipper mood, one saving grace about a busy shift is that it will give me something to distract me from my misery.

I hang my sweater and bag in the back and tie on my apron before heading up front. Nan is busy refilling coffee cups for the people sitting at the counter, but when she sees me she smiles warmly. Then it turns into a frown. "Hey sweetie. Is everything

OK? You look like somebody just drowned your kitten."

Am I that obvious? "I'm fine, just didn't get a lot of sleep last night." Not a lie.

She comes closer and bumps her hip against mine. "Well perk up, buttercup. It's a busy night and there's someone waiting at table nine. He looks like he'll be a real good tipper." She winks and I try not to roll my eyes. I love Nan, but between her and my mother always trying to set me up it gets a little exhausting. Not to mention I'm taken.

Well, kind of.

I grab an order pad and walk over to the table. I don't even bother looking up from the pad when I ask in a fake happy voice, "Do you know what you'd like?"

"As a matter of fact, I do."

As soon as I hear his flirtatious voice my eyes dart up and I almost drop my pen. I couldn't have stopped the giant grin from spreading across my face even if I'd wanted to. "Are you sure it's on the menu?" I ask, trying to hide a relieved smile.

"It better be." Tristan grins devilishly and I have to resist the urge to fling my arms around him and kiss that look right off his face.

"What are you doing here?" I try to remember I'm mad at him. He tends to make me forget that.

"I really had a hankering for pancakes?" He lifts his brow, seeing if I'll buy it. I don't, so he admits, "I didn't want you to be here alone late at night like the last time I was here, but I guess it's a little busier than I remember." He looks around the crowded room.

I chuckle. "Yeah, your timing is a bit off. I don't get off until three."

He looks at me then relaxes back into the booth. "Well then, I guess I'll have those pancakes while I wait."

I try to see if he's joking. "You know that's, like, five hours from now, right? Seriously, Tristan, you don't have to stay. I'll be fine."

"I'm already here." He shakes it off like it's no big deal and adds, "Besides, I think Nan missed me." He grins and lifts a messenger bag from the seat next to him. "I've also got a lot of paperwork to catch up on for work, so I might as well have food and an endless supply of coffee while I do it."

I laugh, not sure how else to react. I'm trying not to read too much into the situation, but Tristan's motives sure are as mysterious as ever. I still want to ask him about a million questions, but knowing he came here just to see me makes it easier to push them aside. At least for now. "I'll be right back with those pancakes, then."

The next few hours pass quickly as I keep busy with my tables. It also doesn't hurt that I have Tristan's presence to distract me. He eats two plates of pancakes and has three cups of coffee before doing some work, but every now and then I catch him looking at me, which makes my lady parts do somersaults.

"THAT POOR BOY LOOKS LIKE he's about to pass out. He should be home in bed at such a late hour." Nan clicks her tongue sympathetically.

"Sorry, he's waiting for me. I told him I don't get out until three but he insisted on staying."

I feel bad when I see Tristan slumped over, his head resting on his arms. He's trying to concentrate on his phone, but his eyes keep slipping shut before they spring back open. I look at the time. It's 1:30 and the crowd just died down for the night. I still have an hour and a half left of my shift. Tristan usually wakes up around three or four in the morning to get to work by five or six, so he's already been up for almost twenty-four hours straight. Would he really risk not getting any sleep just to make sure I wasn't alone?

Before I have time to contemplate the meaning behind that thought, Nan says, "Why don't you take off for the night, hon. I think I can handle the rest of the shift by myself."

I look at her hesitantly. "Really? Are you sure you'll be OK?"

She laughs. "Sugar, I've been doing this longer than you've been alive. I know how to take care of myself. Plus Chet is in the back. Go on now. Get that boy home." She winks and shoos me away.

I smile and remove my apron, then grab my things. When I approach Tristan's table, his eyes are fully closed. I slide in next to him. He jumps awake as soon as he feels my leg press against his.

I try not to laugh. "Sleepy much?"

He stretches, shaking his head. "Nah, just resting my eyes."

"You ready to get out of here?"

He looks at the clock. "What time is it?"

I pick up the truck keys on the table and jiggle them between us. "Time for me to give you a ride." This time I don't try to hide the seductive smile that forms on my lips.

"ARE YOU SURE YOU KNOW what you're doing?"

Tristan's tone is light, but by the way he grips the passenger door handle I can tell he's nervous about me driving his truck. He took his keys back from me before we left the diner, and now he's not giving them up so easily.

I scoff as I buckle myself into the driver's seat. "It's like riding a bike."

Isn't it? It *has* been a while since I've driven a car, but I'm sure it will all come back to me.

Tristan still looks hesitant. "Really, Hazel. I'm not tired."

I hold out my hand. "I promise I won't crash. Come on, you trust me, don't you?"

I smile proudly but it fades when Tristan doesn't smile back. He studies me with a serious stare before putting the keys in my hand.

"Let's see what you've got."

"TOLD YOU I WASN'T TIRED."

Tristan lazily drapes his arm across his stomach, lying back in my bed. We're both naked after having just spent the last hour making each other scream. After I drove us home safely, that is.

I lay my arm over my forehead. "Definitely not tired."

I peek over at Tristan. He catches me looking and smiles, appearing completely contented. I roll on my side to face him, propping my head up on my hand.

"Can I ask you a question?"

His eyes roam down my body. "What kind of question?" He lifts his eyebrows suggestively.

"Seriously, I'm going to need you to focus." I start to pull the sheet up to cover myself.

He quickly grabs for the sheet in protest. "OK, OK. I'll answer your question. But only if you're naked." He grins widely.

I stare at him like he's crazy, but damn if I can resist the excitement in his eyes. If this is the only way he'll talk to me, I'll take it.

I slide the sheet away and let him look his fill, then finally ask, "Why didn't you tell me you own Charter Hill now?"

Tristan's face reveals nothing. "It didn't come up."

I laugh incredulously. "Didn't come up? I asked you if you still worked there."

"And I do." He yawns and looks up at the ceiling. The way he seems completely unfazed frustrates me.

"I'm going to need you to give me a little more than that, Tristan. Please?" My voice ends on a near whisper.

He turns his head to study me, and by the way his brow furrows I get the sense he's debating whether or not he wants to talk. When he looks back up at the ceiling and closes his eyes, my heart sinks. I've pushed too far.

Just as I'm about to roll over to find my clothes, he says, "Honestly, I didn't want you to know." His eyes are still closed and his voice is gruffer than usual.

"Why?"

His eyelids open, but he doesn't look at me. "I guess a part of me didn't think you deserved to know anything about my life now. It was easier not to get into it."

His words sting, but I appreciate the truth. For the first time since reconnecting I feel like Tristan is letting me in, just a small, tiny bit, but the amount of hurt I see in his eyes is almost too much to bear. I know it's because of me, and I wish to God I could take it back.

"Tristan?" I say softly.

"Yeah?"

I look down at the sheet and play with a small thread. I'm scared to ask this next question, probably more scared than I've ever been in my entire life. "I know I don't deserve it, but do you think you can at least try not to hate me anymore? I want us to be friends and we can't do that if you hate me."

I muster all the bravery I can to look back up at his face, but his eyes are closed again. I hold my breath.

After a minute he sighs, His eyelids open. With a piercing gaze he finally answers softly, yet firmly. "I don't make promises I can't keep, Hazel."

His words aren't cruel, just honest. I nod, trying to keep tears from pricking the backs of my eyes. It's now painfully clear I can't fall back in love with Tristan, but that doesn't stop me from needing him. If my body is the only thing he'll take, I'll just have to learn to keep my heart out of it.

I instinctively move to snuggle into his side. I know this isn't something we normally do, since it crosses our clearly defined sex-only line, but right now it doesn't feel like we're Tristan and Hazel: fuck buddies.

Right now we're Tristan and Hazel: two broken people with painful pasts who are each trying to figure out how to heal.

He doesn't pull away, so I have faith that it's at least a start.

STEP FOUR: INTROSPECTION

We made a searching and fearless moral inventory of ourselves.

CHAPTER
eighteen

Hazel

"HAZEL? OH FOR GOODNESS SAKE, are you still sleeping?"

The voice sounds faraway as I try to open my eyes, but immediately shut them again as the bright light shining through the curtains practically blinds me. I bury my face back into the soft mattress.

"Haze—oh my word!" The voice is suddenly much louder.

"Mom?" I croak, lifting my head up, but something heavy and solid weighing on my back prevents me from getting very far.

It moves, and I glance over to see Tristan's naked chest nestled against me, his arm draped across my shoulders.

I roll over and shudder when I realize my mother is standing in the doorway and has just found Tristan and me in bed together. The flurry of movement causes Tristan to sleepily open his eyes, his arm still draped over me.

"Hazel, darling, are you going to introduce me to your guest? It's quite rude not to," my mother says in a clipped, calm tone. I can hear the disgust dripping from every word, but of course she's not going to make a scene. That would be even more improper than walking in on her daughter and a half-naked man.

I groan and sit up, pulling the sheets tighter around my body. Thank God Tristan's junk is covered.

"Mom, you know Tristan, right?" I squeak.

Tristan lazily rolls to his side so he can face her. With a quick lift of his fingers he coolly says, "Hey Mrs. B."

Tristan's hand falls into my lap. I'm literally caught between my uptight, judgmental mother and my laid back, casual fuck buddy.

The stark contrast between them couldn't be more apparent, and if I weren't so mortified, I'd find the situation funny.

My mother crosses her arms and stares at us icily. "I assume that's your vehicle in the driveway, then. With all those tools in the back, I thought it was the gardener's. You do something like that, right? Maybe while you're here you can trim my bushes."

She's too busy being condescending to realize what she said.

Tristan smiles broadly. "If that's what you want, but I've gotta be honest with you Mrs. B, I'd prefer to trim your daughter's."

I subtly pinch his leg under the covers, giving him a death glare, although it probably isn't very convincing, since I can feel laughter bubbling up inside me.

Completely oblivious, my mother continues, "As long as my garden stays pruned, I don't care who you say the bushes belong to. If you leave a card I'll have Julio add you to our service list. You can never have enough help these days."

"Mom!"

It's bad enough she treats me like a child, but does she really have to passive-aggressively insult Tristan, too?

But my outraged frustration falls on deaf ears. "Hazel, when you're done entertaining your . . . *company* here, can I please see you in the parlor?" Her tone leaves no room for argument. She doesn't wait for an answer before turning on her heel and marching out the front door back to the main house.

As soon as she leaves I let out a deep sigh. Tristan just laughs, lying back on the pillows with his hands behind his head. The sheet drapes seductively over his stomach, exposing his chest and arms. A faint shadow of stubble covers his jaw. Despite the unfortunate circumstances, I can't help but notice that his morning voice is throaty and deeply sexy.

"I guess we fell asleep," I muse, choosing not to acknowledge what just happened. When we were younger, Tristan was around enough to understand that there is no explaining the enigma that is my mother. Instead I want to enjoy the idea that Tristan Sharp slept curled around me all night. I don't remember the last time I slept so peacefully, even without any music to help me drift into dreamland.

I look at the clock and see it's just after nine a.m. "Oh my God! You're late for work!"

Tristan stretches, causing the sheet to slip farther down his stomach, revealing his perfectly sculpted right hipbone. It protrudes to form half of a delicious V and I have to resist the urge to bend over and trace it with my tongue.

"Yeah, my boss is going to be pissed." His eyes sparkle. *Sigh.*

A playful Tristan is hot enough at night, but if this is what it's like to wake up to him, too?

Life can be cruel.

Thankfully (or unfortunately), the realization that my mother is currently waiting for me a few yards away, for what I'm sure will be a ridiculously horrifying chat, keeps me from jumping his bones.

"I guess I better not keep my mother waiting. She might come back in here to drag me out."

He grins. "Or maybe she'll just want another peek at all

this." He motions to himself.

I laugh. "God, I hope not." Is it weird that the thought actually makes me kind of jealous?

I grab a tank top from the floor and slip it over my head, trying to keep myself covered with the sheet as much as I can until the shirt is fully on. Last night in the dark I had no problem baring it all for Tristan, but somehow in the harsh light of day I feel overexposed. His eyes are always on me, and I hate that I can never tell what he's thinking.

I just as awkwardly pull on a pair of pants and practically sprint to the bathroom. I can only imagine how I look. Nowhere near as perfect as Tristan, that's for sure.

I brush my teeth and splash some water on my face and by the time I gather enough courage to go back into my room Tristan is fully dressed. *Damn.*

Keys in hand, he points to the door. "I need to get going. I'll talk to you later, OK?"

I nod. After last night, maybe he wants to stop whatever the hell we're doing altogether. I mean he basically admitted he still hates me.

He starts for the door, then turns back to me. I try to not let my face light up like a Christmas tree.

"And Hazel?"

"Yeah?"

"Next time maybe we should stay at my place."

From the way he chuckles I know he's just making a joke, but I don't let that ruin the fact that he admitted there should be a next time.

AS SOON AS I SEE Tristan's truck disappear down the drive I meet my mother in the parlor of the main house.

She's sitting in an olive-colored velvet loveseat, drinking a cup of tea. She doesn't even bother with a greeting as I slump down next to her.

"I talked to Patricia Brattelboro yesterday and she said you haven't returned Thomas' calls."

I close my eyes so she can't see me roll them.

"Mom, I told you I'm not interested."

She studies me. "Because you're too busy traipsing around with gardeners?"

I want to scream. "Tristan is not a gardener! He's a contractor." I cross my arms like a bratty twelve-year-old. "He owns his own business."

I admit I added that last part in the hope that she might see him as more _worthy_ of respect. I hate myself for doing it. I don't want to care about her approval, but I guess a part of me always will. She _is_ my mother, no matter how cruel or hurtful she can be.

But she's either deaf or it doesn't make any difference.

"I never liked that boy. He's bad news. Both him and his brother. But I guess it's not their fault. I mean, what can you expect from children who grow up in foster homes?"

I want to shake her. Knowing I need a second to collect myself before I say something I might regret, I splay my fingers on my thighs and take a few deep, calming breaths. _In . . . 2 . . . 3 . . . 4 . . . 5. Out . . . 2 . . . 3 . . . 4 . . . 5 . . ._

She must be picking up on my discomfort because, in a rare moment of maternal instinct, my mother softens her voice and squeezes my hand. "Hazel, I'm not saying this to upset you. I care about your well being. It won't do any good to get caught up with someone who has had so much heartbreak in his life. I mean, to think his own mother left him and his brother." She shakes her head in pity. "Well, that's unfortunate. Even if she was a drug addict. But being abandoned like that shapes a person, and that's not something you can change. I'm sure he's involved with all sorts of devilish and improper things."

Despite the fact it's drenched in backhanded insults, I'm stunned by my mother's insight. Underneath all that judgment and disdain is something resembling real wisdom. I can't help but wonder if she's thinking about how my father abandoned his own family. What irreversible mark has that left on *us*?

I squeeze her hand back. My mother and I have never shared such a genuine moment.

She retrieves her hand and takes another sip of tea. "Now, Patricia and I decided it's time for Thomas to take you on a proper date. How's tomorrow at seven? He's looking to settle down, you know, so be sure to wear your blue dress."

Moment over.

"Mom," I say gently. "I'm not going to go out with Tommy. I really do appreciate that you're trying to help, but this is something I need to do on my own. I've spent too much time being dependent on other people . . . on other things . . . and it's time for me to figure out my life on my own terms. I need to learn to be OK with *me* before I can even think about adding anybody else into the picture permanently, OK?"

I look her in the eye and pray that what I'm saying will get through to her, that somehow she'll understand.

She cups my cheek in her hand. "OK, dear. Then wear your red dress."

CHAPTER

nineteen

Tristan

"YOU KNOW YOUR APARTMENT IS kinda shitty for someone who runs a construction business."

I can't help but chuckle at Hazel's blunt observation. We're lying on my living room floor talking, bare-ass naked after just having screwed each other senseless all afternoon. A trail of clothes leads from the door to the couch. We didn't make it to the bed. Cutting out of work early was completely worth it.

She adds, "I know money and skill aren't the problem, so care to share?"

I look around and shrug, flashing back to the night Hazel called me to ask for a ride to the baby shower. Didn't the girl I was with then ask me something similar? Hazel's just making meaningless conversation.

When I don't respond right away, Hazel changes the subject. "You know I went on a date last week."

She says this matter-of-factly, and it makes every hair on my body stand on end. Our deal is just sex, so of course she should date if she wants. I shouldn't give a fuck.

I *don't* give a fuck.

"Oh yeah?" I grunt.

"Yup. That doesn't make you jealous, does it?"

Yeah, like I'm going to take the bait. "Why would it?"

I feel her shrug next to me. Since I'm looking up at the ceiling I can't see her face. Probably better this way, because I don't know if it would be worse to see disappointment or relief flash through her eyes. I don't want to know.

But before I can stop myself I ask, "Did you have fun?"

Please say no.

I feel her move beside me. "Nah."

Thank fucking God.

"My mother set me up, so you know it was a disaster right from the start," she explains.

"Anyone I know?"

Shit, I don't want to know.

I'm still not looking at her face, but I somehow can sense she's grinning. "Thomas Brattelboro?" she answers.

"The douche from high school who used to try and pay girls to see their tits?"

"That's the one." She beams.

Rich prick. One time he pissed his pants—literally big, wet spot down the front of his khakis—just because I *threatened* to key his car. I know the dude's a pansy, but suddenly picturing Hazel sitting across from him at some fancy restaurant, offering to whisk her off to the Caribbean on his private yacht, has my stomach in knots. When it's just Hazel and me together I forget how different our upbringing was. She comes from money and I, well, don't.

I've worked hard for each dollar I've ever made, but there's still no way I can compete with the Thomas Brattelboros of the world—in money or status. Sure I own Charter Hill, but running a business isn't always as glamorous as it seems. We do well, but I'm not exactly at wiping-my-ass-with-twenty-dollar-bills status.

Wait, I don't fucking care, remember?

Suddenly very uncomfortable, I try to backpedal. I'd rather talk about my crap apartment than Tommy fucking Brattelboro. "To answer your earlier question, I only use this place to eat and sleep, so why should I waste time making it anything special?"

Hazel rolls on her side to face me, resting her head in the palm of her hand. "But it's still your home. Don't you want it to be special?"

I scoff, surprised she wants more. Like she genuinely cares. "This might be where I live, but it's certainly not a home. Besides, it's meant to be temporary. Or it was, anyway."

"What do you mean?"

For the past two weeks it's become our thing to talk naked after we fuck, and while I wasn't lying when I said I can't promise not to hate her, I have to admit it is sort of nice to be civil. It takes a lot of energy to hate Hazel Blake, especially when I genuinely like being with her. I'm coming to accept the fact that we're friends with benefits—you know, the kind where there actually might be a friend part.

And yes, I have my reasons for not giving two shits about this apartment. Caring would mean it's permanent. That this would be my life until the day I die: a small, shitty apartment with no room for anyone but me.

For now it suits me just fine, but if my entire life consists only of working, eating, and fucking, well then that's pretty fucking sad. Someday I'll figure out what I want to do—who I want to be—and maybe get a dog to keep me company or some shit, but that's sometime far, far, *far* in the future.

Sure, I could add a few throw pillows to this place in the meantime, but that won't change anything. Then it's just throw pillows inside a small, shitty apartment. It'd be like dousing a pile of dog shit in glitter. You can dress it up any way you want, but underneath it's still shit. And what the fuck good is that?

But how do I explain all that to Hazel? Do I want to? What if she just laughs in my face because I'm such a pussy?

It's still uncomfortable for me to express a lot in words, so I figure it's easier just to show her. Maybe it won't be the full story, but I'm trying.

I get up and start putting on my clothes, tossing Hazel's T-shirt and jeans to her. "Come on, I want to take you somewhere."

ABOUT FIFTEEN MINUTES LATER I turn onto a dirt road and cut the ignition. Hazel is quiet for a second before she asks, "What is this place?"

I stare out the windshield at the half-built house. A concrete foundation is poured and most of the wooden frame is up, but there is no roof and the wood is weathered and worn. Grass and weeds climb up and over the concrete, taking over the lot.

We both get out of the car and walk toward the structure, stepping under the wooden beams.

"A few years ago I bought this empty lot with the idea that I'd build a home here."

"What happened?"

What happened? That's a good fucking question. I think for a minute on everything that's happened in my life—everything that's happened between *us*. I couldn't explain it even if I wanted to.

"Fuck, I don't know . . . life?" I pause to look around, kicking at one of the beams. "I started to work on it, but then one day it just didn't seem as important to me. What good is a big-ass house on a huge piece of land when it's just me?"

I watch as Hazel wanders around, taking it all in. She stops at one of the far walls, running her hand over the splintered wood of a giant hole right in the center. She looks fascinated and sad and I start to think it was a mistake bringing her here. What the hell was I thinking?

My phone vibrates in my pocket with an incoming work email and I notice the time: 5:45pm. "Shit, I gotta get going. I have somewhere I need to be."

"Right, it's Thursday. Don't want to keep your *friend* waiting." Hazel smiles, but something about it seems forced.

Her reaction has me confused, not only because I don't know what she's talking about, but also because she sounds jealous. I'm not sure how I feel about that.

"My friend?" I ask.

She waves her hand and starts to turn away. "It's fine, Tristan, really. You don't have to hide it from me. I know you still see other women and I'm cool with it."

I grab her arm and pull her to face me. "Wait, did you just say you're cool with me going to fuck another chick?"

Hazel doesn't say anything, as she looks embarrassed and hurt all at the same time, her eyes saying everything her mouth isn't. For a split second I think that I should confirm her accusation, just to keep things from getting even more complicated between us, but fuck, I can't stand the way she looks like someone just killed her puppy.

"Jesus. All right, let's go. You're coming with me."

Her eyes get wide. "I'd rather not. I might be cool with the fact you're screwing someone else, but I don't need to witness it. And if you think I'm joining in for a threesome you're crazy."

I grin mischievously, unable to resist messing with her just a little. "Good thing there will be four of us, then."

CHAPTER

twenty

Hazel

A FEW MINUTES LATER TRISTAN pulls up to a modest yet charming white cape house with blue shutters and matching door. Doesn't exactly look like the type of depraved sex house I pictured on the way over, but you never know what could be inside.

"You ready?" Tristan turns off the engine and faces me with a grin.

"Ready as I'll ever be," I deadpan.

We walk up the stone path to the front door. Tristan knocks and I try to gulp down a wave of anxiety.

The door opens to reveal . . . *Mr. Turner?*

Wait, what?

Either this is going to be the freakiest orgy of my life, or something else is going on here.

Mr. Turner pats Tristan's shoulder and calls into the house, "Virginia, Tristan's here." His eyes fall on me and he smiles warmly. "And it looks like he brought a friend."

He ushers us inside and I smell the most delicious aroma

wafting from the kitchen. A petite, light-haired woman wearing a red ruffled apron comes around the corner. "There's my guy!" She hugs Tristan before setting her sights on me. "And who's this pretty girl?"

I try not to blush as Tristan introduces me. "This is Hazel Blake." He doesn't clarify further than that.

"She's the one who used to hang around and distract Tristan from work back when he was in high school," Mr. Turner adds. Everyone chuckles.

"Well, then, she's my kind of girl. I keep trying to tell these boys they work too hard, but they never want to listen to me." She moves to hug me, her embrace warm and welcoming, which catches me off guard. "I'm Ben's wife, Virginia, but you can call me Ginny." Ginny puts her right arm around my shoulders and slides her left into the crook of Tristan's elbow, leading us both to the kitchen. "Come on now, dinner is just about ready."

"Whatever it is, it smells amazing," I can't help but gush.

"Why thank you. It's chicken parmesan, my grandmother's secret recipe."

"And my absolute favorite." Tristan chimes in. "But don't bother asking how she makes it, because she won't tell anyone."

As we walk through the kitchen to the dining room, I feel awful that they didn't know I was coming. "I hope it's not too much trouble I came by unannounced."

"Nonsense! Any friend of Tristan's is welcome here any-time. I always make plenty of food and there is a seat at the table right next to him. Now you two go and get settled." She gently scooches us toward the table as she and Mr. Turner get things ready in the kitchen.

Tristan heads straight for one of the chairs and leans back, clearly comfortable in his surroundings.

I position myself in the chair next to him, trying to hide my relief. "So this is where you go every Thursday?"

He tilts his head. "Are you disappointed?"

I try to contain the sheer and utter relief from reading plainly on my face. "It's just not exactly the sex party I thought it'd be."

He grins. "You never know what could happen after dessert."

I stifle a laugh as Mr. and Mrs. Turner enter the room carrying dishes of food. Mr. Turner puts a giant dish of the most mouthwatering chicken parm I've ever seen in my life in the center of the table and Mrs. Turner—Ginny—places a bowl of salad next to it.

Over the course of dinner, which is filled with laughter, stories, and two helpings of food, I discover four things:

1. Mr. and Mrs. Turner are the nicest people I've ever met.
2. This chicken parmesan is my new favorite meal, hands down.
3. Tristan admires the Turners a great deal and they bring out a softer side to him that I really enjoy seeing.
4. I'm completely screwed if I thought I could keep from falling in love with Tristan Sharp all over again.

CHAPTER

twenty-one

Tristan

HAZEL IS QUIET ON THE ride back to my place after dinner. She turned on the radio in my truck and seems perfectly content to sit back and listen to the rhythmic beat as we drive through the dark. Her arm is outstretched next to the passenger window and her head rests lazily against the seat.

I'm not sure how I feel about bringing her to dinner. Nobody knows I go to the Turners' every Thursday night, not even my brother. Other than the whole Hazel situation, it's the only secret I keep from him. My time spent with Ben and his wife has always been the one night I can pretend I have a nice, normal family, and seeing Hazel be a part of that does weird fucking shit to my head. I should have let her think I was off screwing someone else. That would have kept things easy.

She gets to go around dating Thomas fucking Brattelboro like it's no big deal, but the truth is I haven't even looked at another girl since Hazel reappeared in my life—and not for lack of trying, believe me.

Hazel Blake has ruined me for all other women, and for that

I want to make her pay.

I park my truck on the street and we head up the two flights of stairs to my apartment. I unlock the door and let Hazel in first. Needing to regain control, as soon as we enter the dark room and the door slams shut I press myself against her, my front to her back. I drag my tongue along the side of her neck, enjoying how sweet her skin tastes.

She inhales a sharp breath. I feel goose bumps break out across her arms. With my right hand I grab her hip, pulling her tightly against my growing hard-on, and glide my left hand across her stomach, up over her breasts—taking time to pinch each nipple through the thin fabric of her shirt—before sliding my fingers up to grab her chin.

I grip her gently, but firmly, and pull her head back to my shoulder so I can whisper in her ear.

"Do you love it when I touch you?"

I slide my right hand lower, dipping inside her jeans. I brush my fingers over her clit, but pull back until she answers.

"Yes," she breathes, running her hand over my arm.

My fingers push under her panties and slide back to her slit, feeling her slick wetness. She's always so wet for me. So ready for me.

"Do you love it when I own you?" I grunt, circling her opening.

"Yes," she moans, curving her back and spreading her legs wider.

I thrust two fingers deep inside her pussy. They glide in easily. I push them as far as they will go, pressing my palm against her clit to pull her roughly against my now rock-solid dick. I simultaneously move the hand that's on her throat to tangle in her loose hair, twisting it around my fingers so I can pull her head back against my shoulder.

"Do you love it when I hate you?" I challenge, biting her shoulder.

I move my fingers faster, using the weight of my palm to rub every single nerve. When I can feel her getting close to the edge I add a third finger, stroking in and out with a controlling rhythm. Her breath hitches and on a final, explosive moan she cries, "Yes!"

I allow her a moment to ride out the wave, gently stroking her shoulder with one hand as I slowly pull my fingers out of her tight heat, over her clit, and up her stomach.

She covers my right hand with hers and, without letting go, turns around to face me. She continues to drag my fingers up her body, between her breasts, and locks her eyes on mine as she pulls my fingers into her mouth, licking and kissing each one before letting them go.

Light bleeds through the window from the buildings outside, just enough for me to make out her features. Her eyes are dark and wild, her lips pink and perfect. Needing to taste her, I kiss her.

I kiss her hard and I kiss her deep, our tongues colliding between our teeth.

Only when I feel my lungs expand to the point of bursting do I pull back.

I kiss her on the forehead before picking her up in my arms. I carry her to my bed, laying her in the middle.

I pull her clothes off, then mine. Grabbing my phone from my pocket, I put on some soft music. I know she likes that.

I grab a condom from the bedside table and climb over her. I grab her ankles to spread her legs apart, crawling up between them. Her eyes never leave me as she watches my every move.

I sit up on my knees, taking a moment to look at her. To really look at her.

Her hair falls around her shoulders in soft waves. She looks down, almost like she's embarrassed to be seen, but only for a second before she lifts her eyes back to mine. Her tongue darts out to wet her lips, and she looks so goddamn innocent and trusting, like she would do anything I say.

The thought both excites and paralyzes me.

When we're fucking I like to be in control—and she allows it—but the strength in that suddenly feels overwhelming. I'm not sure I can handle the responsibility that comes with this kind of power.

There was a time in my life where I knew with absolute certainly I would never hurt Hazel. And while I would never physically abuse her, or any woman, I'm not so sure I can guarantee that her emotions are just as safe.

There are times, like now, when I look at this girl and want to forgive her for every bit of pain she might have ever caused me.

But then there are times I want to cause her the same kind of deep, twisted pain she inflicted on me. I'm such a sick fuck that I'm afraid one day I will.

But tonight? Tonight I'll allow myself to worship her.

Because as much as I hate her, I also need her.

I already told you, I'm sick.

TWO HOURS—AND THREE ORGASMS—LATER, HAZEL is curled up naked in my bed. I'm lying on my stomach next to her, also naked, with my elbows at right angles and my hands tucked under the pillow my face is buried in. I'm so comfortable I'm about to fall asleep.

Just as my eyes slide shut I feel a soft hand caress my right arm.

An even softer voice asks, "Do they hurt?"

Hazel is on her side facing me. Her fingertips ever so lightly trace the swollen skin of my scars.

"Not anymore," I answer.

"Tristan?"

"Yeah?"

"Will you tell me how you got them?"

Her voice is so gentle, so sincere, so raw. I hold my breath, no longer tired at all. I've never told this story to anyone, but when Hazel and I are together like this—exposed and vulnerable after having consumed each other so completely—I feel powerless to keep up my defenses.

I sigh and turn my head to look at her in the dark. "When I was eight Logan and I were playing hide and seek. I saw my mom leave her room to go downstairs so I decided to hide in her closet. I accidentally knocked over a box. Some needles and shit spilled out. Before I could clean it up my mom came back and found me. She started screaming and threw me back so hard that I fell into her vanity." I try not to cringe as I remember the excruciating pain that tore through my small body. "There was a lit candle on it and the whole thing crashed over landing on top of me. The candle burned my arm and the broken mirror sliced it up."

My eyes have adjusted to the shadows enough to make out Hazel's features—her bottom lip juts out in a frown, but her fingers continue to stroke my arm. For a second it helps. It feels fucking good to say it out loud and have her be the one to hear it.

But I don't want her pity.

I tuck my arms a little further under the pillow and grunt. "She said it was an accident. Probably was."

Hazel pulls her hand back, but doesn't move her body. "You moved to the foster home a few blocks from our house when you were eight."

She phrases it like a statement rather than a question, but I answer anyway.

"Yeah, later that year. Logan and I spent most of our childhood in and out of foster homes. We had actually been in two different ones before we turned six. We would stay there for a bit, but a few months later our mom would take us back home before abandoning us all over again. I guess you only get three chances, though, because after we moved near you, we never went back home."

Hazel scoots closer as she rests her head on the pillow next to me. "You never saw your mom again?"

I roll onto my back to look up at the ceiling. "No, we did. She would come to visit us maybe once or twice a year, when she was sober enough to remember, anyway. When we were about fifteen she got married to some guy who seemed to be a good influence on her. We met him a couple times, and as far as I know they're still together. We don't really keep in touch."

Growing up, there were always rumors about Logan and me. More than once we got into fights because some douche classmate wanted to tease "the loser foster kids." But nobody ever asked us sincerely about our mother or where we came from, so I got used to not saying anything. Hazel doesn't press further now, either, but I can practically hear the million questions forming in her head. I might as well get this out now so we never have to bring it up again. I don't like thinking about it, let alone talking about it.

"Look, my mom was an addict. Heroin was her preferred vice, although I'm sure she wasn't picky. We never knew our dad, but there were plenty of men around to entertain her. She worked two jobs, a convenience store during the day and a bar at night, and we were left by ourselves a lot."

"I'm sure she cared about you." Hazel sounds sincere, but I can tell exhaustion is catching up to her.

"I guess in her own way." I pause, wondering if it's true. I think back as hard as I can to try and remember at least one good memory from my childhood. One time my mom came home early from work and took Logan and me to see a movie. She let us each get our own bucket of popcorn and I remember feeling like the coolest little shit. I saved that bucket for weeks and carried my toys in it. I chuckle to myself at the memory. I haven't thought about that since . . . well, probably since it happened.

"I can't speak for your mom, Tristan, but as someone who once fucked up her own life by thinking being high was the only feeling worth living for, I know how awful it is to later deal with all kinds of regret and self-hatred." Her voice gets heavy as she continues. "But it's hard to give up something that lets you forget all the bad stuff that's happening, especially when it makes you forget to see all the good you have. That's not an excuse, it's just hard. It's hard to face the fact that you have no one to blame but yourself for being so weak. I just want you to know that I bet it hurt her, too. More than you'll ever know."

I want to believe her, but I can't let go of the fact that I still wasn't good enough to keep my mom sober.

That I wasn't good enough to keep Hazel sober, either.

I swallow thickly. "It's hard to feel sympathy when the pain is both selfish and self-inflicted. She made her choice, and that's fine. I can even understand her being weak. But her priorities were clear when she chose drugs over her own sons. So yeah, maybe she cared, but just not enough."

The air shifts and the room goes quiet for a few minutes, except for the soft, sad music still playing in the background.

"I'm sorry, Tristan."

By the way Hazel's voice is barely above a whisper and the

last syllable drops from her lips slowly, I can tell she's falling asleep.

I know she's apologizing because she feels bad about my fucked-up childhood, but something about hearing those exact words at this exact moment feels important.

Rather than feel that usual sick feeling in the pit of my stomach, instead my chest feels tight and I have the urge to wrap Hazel in my arms and kiss her forehead until I fall asleep.

But I don't.

STEP FIVE: ADMISSION

We admitted to God, to ourselves, and to another human being the exact nature of our wrongs.

CHAPTER

twenty-two

Hazel

"THANKS FOR ASKING ME TO grab lunch with you." I smile at Kinsley as she sips her iced tea across the latticed table. We're sitting on the patio of a local cafe downtown.

Kinsley waves her hand. "Thank you for saying yes. Work has been crazy and I needed to get out for a break. I called to see if Kelley wanted to join, but ever since Caden was born she hasn't been getting much sleep."

"Yeah, she and Ryan send me pictures. He's so cute." I smile at the thought of my adorable nephew.

Kinsley puts her glass down, changing the subject. "So how have you been? Anything new? I don't think I've seen you since the DSGN party."

I play with the straw in my cup. "I'm good. Pretty much the same old for me."

"You and Tristan looked like you were getting along," Kinsley says suggestively.

"What? No. I mean, well yeah, I guess . . . We're friends. Kind of. Maybe?" I stutter.

Kinsley just smiles. "Care to elaborate on that?"

I sigh. "OK, fine, but you have to swear not to say anything."

She holds up three fingers, scout's honor style.

"Remember when you asked if we hooked up?" Her eyes sparkle with a hint of *I knew it*, so I continue, "OK yes, we used to have a thing that started back in high school and ended before I went to rehab." I pause, not sure how much of the past I'm willing to share. I look down for a second, then make eye contact and settle for saying, "I . . . well, I hurt him. But ever since the baby shower Tristan and I have agreed on a more casual, physical situation."

"Wait, let me guess: you two are trying the whole friends with benefits thing, right?" Kinsley looks amused.

"I guess you can call it that."

"But you feel something more?"

I shift uncomfortably in my seat, confused by everything that involves Tristan. I honestly don't know what's worse: loving to fuck him, or fucking loving him. And by the way Kinsley is eyeing me, I wouldn't be surprised if all of this was written plainly across my face.

Kinsley looks at me sympathetically before saying, "You know, Hazel, speaking from personal experience, your heart usually wins out in the end. Just saying."

"But that's the thing . . . I don't know if I want it to. What if I'm not capable of change? What if I just end up hurting him again?"

"What makes you think that?"

"First my dad left when I was young, then Ryan hightailed it out of the house as soon as he could, and even though my mother has her *very* rare moments, she's not exactly the most emotionally available person. It must be in the Blake DNA or something, to hurt those around you."

"I think you're being a little hard on yourself," Kinsley says gently.

I shrug, wondering if she knew the whole story, she'd still think that. "Maybe. But it really doesn't matter how I feel, anyway. Tristan made it perfectly clear how he feels, and trust me, he's only in it for one thing."

Kinsley thinks about that for a second. "I know Tristan is a huge flirt and the guy likes to have a good time, but when he's around you I definitely get a different vibe. Hell, all the guys tend to have a rough exterior, but deep down they're big softies."

I think about the undeniable hurt I catch in Tristan's eyes any time we're reminded of the past. My mom was right . . . living with that kind of pain tends to harden a person. I of all people understand that. It doesn't make it any easier that most of it is my fault in the first place. How can he ever move past it, if I'm a constant reminder? I want to be different, for both him and myself, I'm just not sure I can.

But Kinsley is trying so hard to cheer me up and be optimistic that I don't want to be a drag. It's really nice having a friend and I don't want to screw it up with my train wreck of a personal life, so I just smile and truthfully admit, "I sure hope you're right."

"WHAT'S THIS?" I ASK, AS I stare at the paper Tristan just slid across the counter.

It's another late shift for me at the diner, and despite our underlying (mostly unspoken) issues, Tristan and I have fallen into somewhat of a comfortable pattern the last few weeks. I know it's probably not a great idea for me to let myself get in deeper when my emotions are already invested, but ever since I had lunch with Kinsley I guess a part of me really does want to believe that I just need to give Tristan more time. The more we're together, the more I feel the past slip away. It has to be a good sign that we have some type of regular schedule together, right? On the nights I have to work, Tristan will pick me up when he is done at the job site for the day, then he will hang around and catch up on his emails and paperwork while waiting for my shift to be over. Then we'll go back to his place, have sex, and then he'll sleep for an hour or two before dropping me off at home and heading to the office. I worry he's not getting enough sleep, but he says he catches up on the days I don't work.

I squint at the top of the page, not comprehending what I'm reading. It is two in the morning after all, and things just settled down at the diner.

Tristan takes a sip of his coffee before saying matter-of-factly, "It's an application for the Red Cross Certified Nursing Assistant Training Program."

When I alternate between staring at him and the paper, he elaborates. "You once talked about wanting to become a nurse, so I thought this might be a good place to start—get your CNA and see if you like it before deciding your next step."

The fact that he not only remembered me talking about this, but went out of his way to encourage me has me grinning like an idiot. Before I can stop myself I reach across the counter and wrap my arms around him while whispering, "Thank you" into his ear.

When I pull back he says, "You can show me just how appreciative you are later."

He grins and my panties melt right along with my heart.

TWO HOURS LATER, AS I'M staring at a spent and satisfied Tristan Sharp lying naked on my bedroom floor, I think I did a good job of proving just how appreciative I am.

I practically mauled him as soon as we left the diner, and since I know my mother will be away at a spa for a few days, and my place is a little closer than his, we ended up here.

He looks up at the ceiling with wide eyes. "That thing you did with your . . . and my . . . *wow.*" He lets out an astonished, satisfied sigh.

I peek over the edge of my bed and giggle. "You're welcome," I beam from directly above him.

Tristan closes his eyes, looking like his mind has been thoroughly blown. I admire how perfect he is, and wish I could keep this moment . . . keep *him* . . . forever.

I reach over and grab my Nikon from the desk. I hold it out in front of me, putting one eye to the viewfinder while squinting the other shut. I focus on his strong, square jaw and frame it with a portion of his delicious lips. A small nick is present right at his jawline, probably a cut from shaving. I press the shutter, which produces a soft *click*.

Without opening his eyes, Tristan smirks. "See something you like?"

"Mhmm," I breathe, zooming in on his long eyelashes that rest gently over his pinch-able cheeks. For the first time I notice the mild swelling and gray tint under his eyes, no doubt from lack of sleep. *Click.*

"Open your eyes for me," I softly command. He obeys without question, and as soon as his big, brown eyes come into focus, I snap another picture. They shine with amusement, but I can't help but notice the hint of torment buried deep inside them.

He reaches out and I let him pull me from the bed. He positions me to straddle him, a leg on either side of his well-defined stomach. His hands grip my thighs, his calluses a proud symbol of all of his hard work. *Click.*

I next aim the camera toward his right arm, capturing the pale yet toughened skin that is a physical reminder of all his suffering. I bend down and press a soft kiss to each mark.

Tristan tucks his arms behind his head, puffing out his chest so he's fully bared to me. "I'm sure there's another part of me you're just dying to document." He grins and flexes his hips, pressing his growing hard-on against my ass.

I exhale an excited breath and slide down his body to line him up at my entrance. *Click.* He reaches across the floor to his jeans and pulls out a foil packet. *Click.* He rolls the latex down his thick, impressive length. *Click.*

He grabs himself with one hand, steadying me with his other. I balance on my knees over him as he rubs against my slick core. *Click.*

Right before he pushes inside me, he takes the camera from my grasp. He holds it to his face with one hand, keeping the other planted firmly on my hip.

I arch my back and slide onto Tristan's cock at the same moment he thrusts upward. I hear the steady tempo of a *click, click, click,* accompanying my rhapsodic moans.

Needing to taste him as much as I feel and see him, I lean forward to press my lips firmly against Tristan's as I ride him, powerfully and intensely. He stretches his arm out to the side, angling the camera to capture the meeting of our mouths. *Click.*

I buck my hips faster and harder, reveling in our naked display of pure, unadulterated passion. It's the most erotic experience of my entire life, and I've never felt so raw, so *seen.*

So beautiful.

I wrap my arms around Tristan's neck, holding us together.

When his lips brush my ear and I hear him whisper, "Let's come for the camera, baby," every fiber of my being melds with his and we explode in perfect unison, our bodies emptied and aching amidst a barrage of *clickclickclicks*.

Although I barely hear the sound of the camera, because the pleasure ringing in my ears is almost deafening. I collapse onto Tristan's broad, heaving chest. I stay there until my world stops spinning.

When I finally roll off him to curl into the crook of his shoulder, the steady beating of his heart makes me feel at peace. I hear him place the camera on the floor with a gentle *thud* and he reaches for a tissue to quickly clean himself up. When he's finished he wraps one arm lazily around me, kisses my forehead, and falls fast asleep.

After a few minutes I gently slip out of his grip, careful not to wake him. I grab my camera off the floor and crawl to the opposite side of the room. I adjust my lens to zoom out, framing Tristan's entire body. I take my final picture of the night as I inhale a shaky breath.

Pieces of this man may be flawed, but as whole, he is perfect.

CHAPTER

twenty-three

Ten years ago

Tristan

"TRISTAN! YOU MADE IT, BRO. Hey, I was just telling these guys about the time we totally wrecked the Smith brothers in that basketball game. They were practically in tears. I sure am going to miss high school."

Logan throws his arm around one of our classmates as a few others laugh. They're all wasted beyond belief, celebrating our graduation, but I don't have time to deal with them. I need to find Hazel.

We were supposed to meet at our spot an hour ago, and when she didn't show I knew she'd be here instead. She's been blowing me off more and more lately, and it's all that fucker Dougie D's fault.

For the past year Hazel and I have gotten a lot closer, but I still can't seem to stop her from doing drugs. I've tried to reason with her but she refuses to acknowledge she even has a problem, and I can't approach Ryan because he's usually so shit-faced himself I'm not sure he's in a position to think clearly. He already thinks I'm involved in this shit, too, but there's no point in arguing with a drunk Ryan Blake. Not to mention he'd kick my ass if he found out I deflowered his sister. Not knowing how else to help her, I've been trying to keep her distracted by hanging out with her at our secret spot, but lately I can feel her slipping farther and farther away.

Ignoring my brother's drunken enthusiasm, I look around the crowded room for any sign of Hazel. This wouldn't be the first time I have to pull her out of a party.

Not seeing her in the living room or the kitchen, I head down the hallway and start checking all the rooms. I'm having a serious flashback to the last time I found her here—she was wearing a too-tight black dress, snorting lines with Dougie, and when I tried to get her out she screamed at me.

When I finally get to the last door, I hear someone laughing on the other side. I don't even hesitate.

What I find makes me want to throw up.

Hazel is lying on the bed, topless, and Dougie is bent over her with his pants around his ankles. His dirty, disgusting dick is in his left hand while his right moves under her skirt. Two guys are sitting on the other side of the room, getting high and watching with a nauseating air of amusement.

Before I know what's happening I'm tackling Dougie to the ground, screaming "Get the fuck off her!" as I bash my fists into his face.

Hazel tries to pull me off him, yelling, "Stop, Tristan, Stop!" over and over again.

All of a sudden I feel another set of fists pummeling my back and am surprised when I see they're Ryan's. Considering Hazel is half-naked and crying for me to stop, I can see how he might get the wrong idea, but that shit is going to have to wait—I have another asshole to deal with, first.

I shrug Ryan off, which isn't hard since he's obviously tanked. He falls drunkenly to the ground.

Only when Dougie's face begins to look as bloody and battered as raw meat—and my hand screams in pain—do I relent.

I grab Hazel's shirt off the floor and press it to her so she can cover herself up. When it's on I grab her arm and, without looking back, pull her through the party and out to my car. I peel out of the driveway so fast a cloud of smoke billows behind us.

I don't say anything as I pull into our secret spot and cut the ignition. My jaw hurts from how hard I clenched it the entire ride here.

I'm so fucking pissed and heartbroken and sick about the entire situation that I'm afraid I might lose it.

But when I look over and see Hazel curled into a ball against the passenger door, tears streaking her face, my anger melts away.

I gently reach my hand out to brush her shoulder. "Are you OK?"

She sniffles and looks at me with regret in her eyes. "I'm sorry. I don't know what I was thinking. I . . . I . . ."

She drops her head and her shoulders convulse in sobs. I reach around and pull her as close as I can to my chest. "It's not your fault, Hazel. That asshole should have never put his hands on you. I swear to God I wanted to kill him. I should have."

She sobs louder before shifting to look at me. "But it is my fault. I let him do it, Tristan."

I shake my head in protest, but Hazel nods, seeming embarrassed as she looks to her lap. She sniffles again before admitting, "My mom and I had another fight. She told me I have no chance at a future, that nobody will ever want me. I just wanted to forget everything for a while so I went to the party looking for Dougie. I didn't have any money with me, so he suggested another way for me to pay."

I squeeze my eyes shut as a fire burns in my chest, fueled by disappointment, guilt and torment.

"It was stupid, I know. I'm sorry, Tristan, I really am. But please, please, you can't tell Ryan. You can't tell anyone. I can't let them know how stupid I am. Please. They can't ever know I'm such a fuck-up that I'm willing to have sex for drugs. Please promise you won't tell anyone."

Her begging guts me and it takes everything in me to nod in agreement. I would do anything for Hazel. Hell, I blame myself for agreeing to let her meet me tonight. I should have picked her up so she never would have been in this situation in the first place.

"I'll never tell anyone." She looks relieved to hear me say that. "But you have to promise me you're done with that fucking shit, Hazel. I mean it. I'll always be here for you and I swear I'll do everything I can to find a way out for us, but I need you to be done with this." I convince myself I'm doing this solely for her own good, but the really fucked up part is I think I'm also asking for me. I know I can't ever truly call Hazel mine while she's addicted to something else.

Tears continue to roll down her cheeks as she whispers, "I promise."

I hug Hazel closer to me and as she cries on my shoulder I make another promise to myself—a promise that one day I will be able to offer Hazel a future.

A future for us both.

I START TO PACK UP my tools when I'm done framing the windows on the Johnson property. CJ and Brent have already packed up so they nod goodbye. When I head out to my car a few minutes later, I'm surprised to see Ryan leaning against it. He looks like he hasn't slept in days.

We haven't talked much in the three months since . . . well, since the night I won't ever forget. The image of Hazel about to get fucked by that asshole is forever burned into my brain. As much as I hate it, it's at least fueling me to keep my promise of a better life for us. Since I graduated and don't have school to deal with I've been taking every extra shift Mr. Turner will give me, saving up as much money as I can. I don't have a plan yet, but I know it will take a lot of hard work and sacrifice no matter what it is.

Ryan, in his drunken, fucked-up mind, chooses to believe I was the one who got Hazel hooked on coke in the first place, claiming he saw my sorry ass every time Dougie D was around his sister. That second part is probably true since I was trying to keep her away from Dougie, and the only way to do that was to hang around where she was. A few times Ryan even tried to drunkenly fight me because of it. But in terms of the first part? Well, Ryan sees what he wants to see, and apparently I'm just a no-good druggie. Like mother like son, right? Since he's usually too drunk to know his ass from his mouth, it's no use trying to set the record straight anymore.

"You look like shit," I muse, brushing past Ryan to throw open the back door of my car. I toss my tools on the back seat and slam the door shut. I wouldn't be surprised if he's already hammered and just wants to get on my case again.

Ryan shoves his hands in his pockets, unamused. "Gee, thanks. I didn't come here for your warm and fuzzy compliments, though."

I run my fingers through my hair. "Then why the fuck did you come here?"

He looks off into the distance and I notice his expression, while distant, is focused. For the first time in a long time I think he's actually sober.

He toes a rock on the ground with his shoe before looking back at me. "I know I haven't exactly been in the best place lately, so I'm going to get help. There's a rehab center that specializes in alcoholism so I'm going to be away for a while. I need to get better if I have any chance of doing something good with my life."

"Shit," I mutter, both shocked and impressed. Ryan Blake is nothing if not proud, so for him to admit this, especially to me, is a huge step in itself.

He nods. "Yeah. But before I go I wanted to talk to you. I want to make sure you're going to stay away from Hazel while I'm gone. In fact, I want you to stay away from her for good."

I scoff. Of course. This again. "Look, man, I told you a million times, I'm just looking out for her. That night . . . what happened . . ."

I shake my head, unable to find the right words. "It's not what you think."

I see Ryan's jaw tic and I know he's trying really hard not to lose his temper with me. "Let me guess, you were all just having a tea party, right?" He laughs sarcastically. "I'll be the first to admit I don't remember a whole hell of a lot of details, but I sure as shit know my sister was half-naked and screaming in a room with a bunch of coke heads, and you were in the middle of it all. Unless you can give me a good reason for any of that shit, I think I have all the info I need."

I study Ryan's face. How easy would it be to tell him the truth? If he only knew what was really going on that night, maybe he wouldn't hate me so much.

But I remember promising Hazel I wouldn't say anything, and I know I'll keep her secret until the day I die. I also know hearing the truth would only break Ryan's heart, possibly even more than mine. To hear that his baby sister was willing to whore herself out in order to get high? What good would that do either of them? Especially now that he's finally going to get the help he needs. I don't want him to have this hanging over his family. No, let him blame me. Let him hate me. I'd rather he look at me with all the disdain and disappointment in the world, rather than think less of Hazel.

Besides, he's also right in a way. Any way you slice it, nothing about what went down that night should have happened in the first place. I knew Hazel had a problem and didn't pay enough attention to how much trouble she could get in, so it's just as much my fault for not being able to save her.

I settle for telling him the only part of the truth I can, hoping it will at least salvage some part of our friendship. "You're right. I shouldn't have let her get into that mess. And for that I'm sorry. But you have to believe me, man, I didn't touch her. I'd never hurt Hazel."

He narrows his eyes at me, trying to tell if I'm feeding him a line of bullshit. He must know I'm telling the truth because after a long pause he says, "I know you wouldn't do that. But I still don't like the idea of you around her, OK? You have to understand that."

I nod, understanding exactly what he means.

I'm also really fucking glad he didn't make me swear to stay away from her, because that is one promise I know I won't be able to keep.

CHAPTER

twenty-four

Tristan

"ARE YOU SURE THIS KID is Ryan's? He's a lot cuter than Ry is."

"They do have the same shit-eating grin."

"Dude, I think it's a shit-making grin."

Logan waves his hand in front of his face and we both take a step back. Yup, this little man definitely just took a dump.

Caden Brooks Blake was born seven weeks ago, and while I usually find babies pretty gross—case in point, the load he just dropped in his diaper—I think this could be the one kid I actually like.

Caden smiles up at me from his basket thing as if to say, *Yup, I might stink, but I'm cute so I can get away with it.*

"Kelley, I think your kid needs to be changed. And from the smell of it you might need a Hazmat suit," I quip from across the lawn.

"That's my boy." Ryan beams, causing everyone to laugh.

Ryan and Kelley invited a bunch of us to the local park for an afternoon cookout as a sort of casual baby-welcoming slash post-wedding celebration, since they eloped a few weeks ago. I was surprised to hear that Ryan actually locked that shit down, but I have to admit things now seem different between him and Kelley. Not that I'm an expert, but the dude really seems to love the girl.

I apologized to them both about the whole baby shower incident and Kelley insisted the whole thing was a misunderstanding and forced us to make peace.

I look around the park and notice everyone milling about, shooting the shit about this and that. I catch Hazel's eye from a few feet away. She's standing by the picnic tables with a group of four other people I don't recognize. Hazel appears to be on the outskirts of the conversation, nodding every once in a while, but not really paying attention. She's wearing a flowy yellow dress that falls about mid-way down her thigh. When the breeze picks up it lifts just enough to torment me. I want to walk right up and slide my hand under there, but I know I can't.

Hazel took the bus here today, not wanting to arouse suspicion—or piss off Ryan again—by arriving with me, so I haven't gotten the chance to talk to her. It's been a few days since we've seen each other and I'd be lying if I said I didn't want her, right here, right now.

I look over to see Kelley and Ryan busy with the baby, so I casually make my way over to where Hazel is standing. I, too, make it look like I'm interested in whatever it is these assholes are saying. Before I turn to leave, I lean in to whisper in Hazel's ear, "Meet me behind the pavilion in five."

Hazel doesn't make any public acknowledgement of what I say, but by the way she holds back a smirk and goose bumps form on her arms despite the summer heat, I know she'll do it.

A few minutes later she comes around the corner of the stone pavilion, which blocks us from the rest of the crowd. She opens her mouth to say something, but I push her up against the stone wall and kiss her hard and fast. She tries to resist, but only for a second before she melts against me, meeting my own animalistic desire. I reach my hand to slide my fingers against her thigh, and fuck if it isn't just as soft as I imagined it. I slide my finger further and further up her dress, but right before I reach between her legs she stops me.

"Mmm, we can't." She whispers into my mouth, still kissing me between her words.

I grind myself harder against her. "Why not?" I run my tongue down her neck while my fingers tease up and down her leg.

""'Cause . . . well . . . mmm . . . there are kids around!" She giggles breathlessly, clearly conflicted.

I groan, but pull back. I would take her up against this wall right now without any fucks given as to who sees, but I also don't want to scar some poor innocent child for life. I'm not a monster.

I rest my forehead against hers, trying to will my dick to settle down. He, apparently, *is* a monster. "Fine, not here. Tonight? My place?"

Hazel smiles, nodding in agreement.

"You get back to the party first. I need a minute." I lean against the cool stone, attempting to prevent the worst case of blue balls imaginable from forming.

Hazel laughs, clearly not understanding the torture, because it's anything but funny. "I'll help you with that tonight."

"You better," I say on an agonized grunt.

"Well, if you're good." She laughs again and kisses me before disappearing around the corner.

CHAPTER

twenty-five

Hazel

I HEAD BACK UP TO the party, feeling deliciously dizzy from a combination of the sun's heat and Tristan's touch.

I slip back into the crowd, praying nobody noticed our absence. A few minutes later Tristan does the same, looking much less affected than he did when I left him.

I blush, thinking about what we almost just did, and try to keep myself from pulling him back behind the pavilion for the rest of the afternoon.

After things wind down and just about everyone has left, Ryan asks, "Do you want us to give you a ride home?"

Tristan pops out of nowhere. "I can do it. That way you can get your little guy home." I didn't realize he had stayed, but I'm excited he did.

"It's fine. We'll take her." Ryan's voice is calm, but by the way he refuses to make eye contact with Tristan I can tell he's pissed.

"I don't mind," Tristan responds easily.

The two guys stare each other down while I watch in

disbelief, getting pissed myself.

"Um, hello. Remember me? The girl who is old enough to decide things for herself?" I cross my arms, looking between them.

Without even bothering to look at me Ryan says, "Stay out of this, Hazel. I'm just looking out for you."

That makes me laugh, even though I don't find it particularly amusing. "Looking out for me? Seriously? Just because you're a father now doesn't mean you're *my* father. I'd rather go with Tristan than you, but thanks anyway."

"I don't want you going anywhere with him,"

"You know I wouldn't let anything happen to her." Tristan finally steps in, his voice sounding soft and sincere in comparison to our tenser tones.

If Ryan notices, he doesn't care. "Screw you, Sharp. I want you to stay away from my sister. I told you that in high school, but you seem to have forgotten. Do I have to remind you what happened? What *you* let happen to her?" Ryan clenches his fists at his sides, looking like he wants to punch Tristan's lights out.

Tristan looks like he's about to do the same right back, but doesn't move. I know exactly what he's thinking—that he's honoring my secret and would take any abuse Ryan has to give in order to keep his promise.

It's suddenly clear to me just how much my brother blames Tristan for my past, and my heart bleeds to realize Tristan has let him all these years. Even though he hated me, Tristan never betrayed me.

And I finally need to make this right.

I step in front of Tristan to face Ryan. "It's time you knew the truth."

Tristan steps up right behind me and grabs my shoulder. "Hazel, don't."

For a split second I want to listen to him. To feel his warm, safe arms wrap me up and shield me from the truth. It would be easier than admitting my own fucked-up mistakes.

But I steel myself. No, Tristan deserves the truth. I deserve it, too.

"I said get away from her."

Ryan takes a threatening step closer, but I hold up my hand and yell, "It's not Tristan's fault! I know you think it is, and I've let you for far too long. That night was my fault, Ryan, all of it. Everything was my fault." I try to hold them back, but a few tears escape down my cheeks. "I chose to go to that party by myself and I agreed to have sex with Dougie in exchange for getting high."

I pause, letting the truth sink in.

The horror shows plainly on Ryan's face, but he needs to hear it all. "Tristan showed up to stop me. That's why he was there, Ryan. He never did drugs and it wasn't his fault. He saved me. He was always trying to save me."

I glance at Tristan, admitting the next part with my eyes locked on his. "He stood by me when nobody else did and he's the only person in my life who's never left me."

Tristan's eyes dilate, but he makes no other move. I blink away more tears and focus back on my brother. "He loved me, Ryan. He cared for me and he tried to keep me safe and he _loved_ me. And I loved him back. I still do."

Ryan looks shocked, angry, sad, and disappointed all at once, clearly not knowing what to say. But that's OK. He doesn't have to say anything. This was for Tristan. This was for me.

The tears are full on pouring out now, but I don't move. I stand still, allowing myself to feel every single emotion of this moment. I feel Tristan's hand slip into mine, anchoring me to be strong as he gently pulls me toward the parking lot, away from the aftershock of the truth bomb I just detonated.

STEP SIX: ANTICIPATION

We were entirely ready to have God remove all these defects of character.

CHAPTER

twenty-six

Tristan

I GET HAZEL INTO THE car and start to drive. I drive fast and far and I keep driving us farther and farther away from whatever the fuck just happened.

All I saw and all I heard was the bravery in Hazel's confession, and it fucking obliterated me. So I don't know where we're going, but I know it needs to be far away from here.

We ride in silence for twenty minutes. When Hazel finally speaks, her voice is soft and though she's sitting upright, her shoulders are hunched. It's as if it's literally taking everything she has to stay strong. She looks small, but resilient. No signs of weakness. "Where are we going?" she asks.

"Anywhere that isn't here."

Hazel doesn't acknowledge my answer, but she doesn't question it either.

After another forty minutes the sun is setting as I pull up to a quiet, secluded house situated right next to the ocean.

I turn off the engine and get out. I help Hazel do the same. We walk up the narrow path that leads around the back of the house to a private beach.

Hazel looks around, wrapping her arms around her shoulders. "What is this place?"

I come up behind her. "Mr. Turner owns it. He and his wife come up sometimes, but a few years ago they gave me a key. In exchange for helping with a lot of the upkeep, I can come here anytime I want." I choose not to tell her that this has become my new secret spot—the place I come to get away when life feels like it's too much. Logan and I actually bought our own beach house a few years ago—a party pad more than anything—but this is the place that feels safe.

"It's so peaceful. I like it."

Hazel's voice is soft and faraway, and I can tell there is a lot weighing on her mind.

There's a lot of shit I'm confused about, too, but right now I just need to be with her.

I grab her hand, silently leading her to the back door, and insert a key into the lock. When the door clicks open, I nudge it and pull Hazel inside. The door doesn't even fully close before I have her pressed against it, slamming it shut with the weight of my body on hers. My lips and hands are everywhere at once. I know she's confused. I know we should talk. But right now I want to forget anything exists outside of us. For this brief moment of bliss the world doesn't have to make sense. I don't have to worry about the past or think about the future.

It's just us.

Tristan Sharp.

And Hazel Blake.

Fucking.

Because that's the only thing that makes sense between us.

It's the only thing I know how to do.

CHAPTER
twenty-seven

Hazel

I'M PRESSED AGAINST THE DOOR with Tristan's body against mine, his hands digging roughly into my skin, his mouth stealing all the air from my lungs.

It's wild and messy and it's never felt more right.

I kiss him back just as hard, needing him to consume me, to fill me.

His mouth makes its way across my neck, down my breasts, branding me with every touch. He finds his way back to my lips and pulls me away from the door, his mouth never breaking contact with mine. We fall to our knees. Tristan reaches for my clothes while I reach for his. He pulls my yellow dress over my head. I pull his white shirt over his.

He kisses the spot below my throat while unclasping my bra, letting it fall away. He palms my breasts with his strong, callused hands. I surrender to him, arching into his touch, moaning and begging for him to fuck me.

Instead he stops.

He looks at me in the growing darkness, the sun barely

peeking in the windows as it sets. Harsh shadows slice across his face and everything stands still. He stares at me, quietly and deliberately.

His body might be rough, but his eyes are gentle. He's the only person to ever look at me like I actually mean something.

And for the first time I honor the silence. In fact, I welcome it.

Tristan's left hand relaxes at my hip while his right slides behind my neck, pulling me close.

He's still staring at me, silently saying more than any words ever could. The intensity causes me to inhale a sharp breath. The rise and fall of my chest pressed against Tristan's makes me even more aware of how electric his bare skin feels next to mine.

He angles his face closer, but just when I think he's going to kiss me he pulls back. He instead shifts to lay me gently on the floor. Once he makes sure I'm comfortable on my back, he oh-so-slowly trails his fingers from my neck down my sides and slides my panties down my legs. He pushes himself to standing and unbuttons his jeans, his eyes never once leaving mine. I watch as he steps out of his pants and rolls on a condom. I watch him kneel in front of me. I spread my legs to allow him to climb over me and he holds his weight on his hands. He puts his forehead against mine.

The sun has fully set and it's just the two of us. Nothing else matters. Not where we are or who we used to be or what anyone else thinks.

"Did you mean what you said?" His voice is low and gruff.

"Yes." I don't have to ask what he's talking about.

With my admission Tristan finally closes his eyes. He doesn't say anything back. I can feel his body tense, but I can't tell if it's good or bad. He doesn't move, and I'm gripped with an overwhelming fear that I just lost him. He's not ready. It's OK if he's not ready to love me again. I just need to feel him. That's where we make sense. It hurts to face the truth of all the pain I've caused, but it hurts even more to think of losing him.

I hold onto his shoulders and try to hold back tears as I whisper, "Tristan? Will you please fuck me? You don't have to love me. Just please, take the hurt away."

His eyes fly open and the previous calm is replaced by something else. An urgency. A need.

He digs his fingers into my hips before pushing quickly, deeply, and fully inside me. I cry out not from pain or displeasure, but from the shock of how complete I feel. They say two wrongs don't make a right, but somehow we do. For as much as Tristan and I can't be together, we're made for each other.

I squeeze my eyes shut and bury my face in Tristan's shoulder, holding on to every piece of him he's ever given me. I hold on to the hope that, despite all odds, this might somehow be a new beginning for us. I hold on to that hope because it's all I have left.

In this moment we are everything—fear, love, history, pain—held together only by truth.

The kind of truth you can only tell in the dark.

The kind of truth that will change everything.

STEP SEVEN: PAIN

We humbly asked Him to remove our shortcomings.

CHAPTER

twenty-eight

Five Years Ago

Tristan

"HERE YOU GO, SON. *I have to say you're probably the youngest landowner I've ever met. Must be in a hurry to grow up or something.*"

The real estate agent, Mr. Jenkins, hands me the final signed deed to the lot I just bought.

"*Just excited to start my life and provide for my family, sir.*" I reach my hand out to shake his.

"*Family, huh? You're not married or something, are you?*"

I smile. "*Not yet.*"

I PULL UP TO HAZEL'S house and take a calming breath before getting out. I don't want to give the surprise away as soon as she sees me.

Our relationship may not have been official up to this point, but that's only because we've been stuck. We knew telling anybody about us would only lead to more drama, so we agreed that until we had a way out, we'd stick to our secret hookups.

For the past five years I've been working day and night at Charter Hill to save up money so we could have a fresh start. In the same amount of time, Ryan put himself through law school, Logan and Lucas started up some crazy venture capital firm, and, ever since her senior year, Hazel has taken an interest in photography. Even though we barely get to see each other and our patience has been tested, she's managed to stay clean just like she promised. I knew she could do it if she really wanted to, and a part of me even likes to think she did it for me, too. For us. I'm so proud I could burst. It hasn't been easy putting our lives on hold, but I can finally see a light at the end of the tunnel.

I finally have our way out.

I fold up the deed and put it in my inside jacket pocket, right next to the small velvet box already there. I try to contain my excitement as I let myself inside. Her mother is out tonight, so Hazel and I should have a couple of hours alone.

I head up to Hazel's room but the door is closed. I knock and when Hazel opens it I can immediately tell something is up.

"What are you doing here?" She looks surprised to see me.

I furrow my brow in confusion. "I told you I was coming by, remember?"

She looks up as if trying to recall, then shrugs. "Oh, right. Did you need something?" She grips the door, sandwiching herself between it and the frame like she doesn't want to let me inside. Her eyes dart back and forth and I notice her pupils are dilated.

My stomach rolls.

"Are you fucking high right now?" I don't wait for an answer before pushing the door open to reveal two guys and a girl sitting on the floor, along with a mirror and a rolled-up twenty-dollar bill.

I get a sick, sinking feeling that I don't know who this girl is at all. It can't be my Hazel—she promised. How long has she been lying to me?

I grab a small bag of white powder off the floor and stare at Hazel in disbelief. "I thought you told me you were done with this shit?"

Hazel crosses her arms defensively. She looks hollow and weak. "Maybe I just told you what you wanted to hear."

I clench my jaw and stare down the three people still on the floor. I point to the door with my free hand and say through gritted teeth, "Party's over. Get the fuck out." When they aren't moving fast enough, I yell, "Now!"

As they stumble out, Hazel tries to fight me. "It's my fucking life, Tristan. I can do whatever the hell I want!"

"It was supposed to be OUR life!" I yell, unable to control my emotions. This only agitates her more in her drugged-up state, so I try to calm us both down.

I grab her hands in mine, stopping them from pummeling my chest. "Babe, please. Listen to me. You don't need to do this. We can get out of here and start our own life together. It's us against the world, right?"

I put my forehead against hers, trying to reach her. For a second she melts into my arms and I think I've got her, but just as quickly she's pulling away.

"You don't fucking get it! It's not us against the world, Tristan, it's the world against us."

"We can get through it together."

"Together? You think because we fuck once in a while we're together? We're nothing, Tristan. I'm nothing to you and you're nothing to me."

I search her face, looking into her cold, wild eyes. She's just mad at me. She doesn't mean it. "I love you. I'm in love with you, Hazel. I want to spend the rest of my life with you."

"You can't be serious right now." She laughs cynically.

I reach for the box in my pocket to show her just how serious I am.

I hold the black box in one hand, the white bag in the other. "You can choose which way you want your life to go right now, Hazel. But *it's one or the other. You can't have both."*

She looks at me with an expression I can't read. Her eyes are either sad or sorry and I hold my breath, scared shitless to find out which it is.

Her hand slowly lifts before grabbing the white bag.

STEP EIGHT: PUNISHMENT

We made a list of all persons we had harmed, and became willing to make amends to them all.

CHAPTER
twenty-nine

Tristan

I WAKE UP IN A cold sweat. I haven't had a dream about that night in years.

I look over and see Hazel sprawled across the pillow next to me.

The girl that finally said she loves me.

Maybe I just told you what you wanted to hear. I get that sinking feeling in the pit of my stomach.

I roll out of bed and leave the room, quietly shutting the door behind me. I find my clothes by the door where we came in last night and pull them on. I look at the clock—it's 6:13 in the morning. Still early. I slip out the back door.

As I walk along the deserted beach behind the house I think about my life. I think about how I grew up and how my mom treated me like garbage, about how Logan and I were bounced around foster homes, feeling like we were never wanted. I think about meeting Hazel and growing up and falling in love with her. I think about the night she chose drugs over a life with me and I think about how much I hated her for it. I think about fucking countless nameless, faceless girls for the past five years. I think about how much I wanted to get back at Hazel the minute I saw her name flash on my cell phone, for destroying any good I used to have in me.

Do I love Hazel Blake? Fuck, I don't know. Can you love somebody you hate? We've been through hell and back and I'd be lying if I said I didn't get some sick pleasure out of fucking her.

But last night? That wasn't fucking, even if it's what she asked of me. Our arrangement was supposed to be simple—sex and only sex—yet what we did suddenly feels very complicated.

The thing is, I don't want to hurt her. Maybe a part of me did in the beginning, but not anymore. I can tell she's different now and I want her to have her second chance. It just can't be with me—I'm more fucked up than ever. This whole time I've been telling myself I never knew the real Hazel, but the truth is I know Hazel better than I know myself sometimes. And that thought terrifies me. If I stay with her I'm afraid I'll lose myself again, only to give her the chance to break us all over again. I can see now how leading her on has only caused more pain. It's time to man up and make amends for that. I was weak, to give into her temptation, and now I'm left to suffer the consequences. I need to end this so we can both move on.

Even if I wanted to, I don't know how to love Hazel Blake. And if I can't love her I need to leave her. For good this time.

CHAPTER
thirty

Tristan

WHEN I GET BACK TO the house Hazel is in the kitchen, awake and dressed in yesterday's clothes. She smiles when she sees me and my chest fucking burns, making it hard to breathe.

"Hey, I was wondering where you were. I thought you abandoned me here or something." She laughs playfully and moves around the kitchen island toward me, but I turn away like a coward. I can't bear to see her look so happy—not if I'm the reason for it.

"Tristan? Is everything OK?"

She gently holds onto my arm and I close my eyes. *Why does her hand have to feel so fucking good?* My fists clench and I muster every single ounce of detachment I can.

I look at her blankly and blurt, "We need to end this."

She furrows her brow and bites her lip and I hate that I still want to reach out and kiss it. Her arms fall to her sides and she stands motionless, staring at me in a way that says she is hurt, yet not surprised.

What feels like several long minutes pass before she speaks

softly, with a single tear running down her cheek. "I don't want there to be an end to us."

Gutted.

Wrecked.

Ruined.

Every piece of my heart shatters at the pure and simple truth pouring from her, but I steel myself, knowing that we need an end if I want her to have a new beginning. "There is no *us*. I made it perfectly clear that the only thing we've been doing is fucking."

I suddenly regret ever having wished any sort of revenge on Hazel. It's like I see myself standing back in her room, except this time it's me choosing the white bag over the black box. The pain might be the same either way, but at least my choice isn't selfish. I'm doing this so she can finally move on.

At least that's what I tell myself.

I expect Hazel to walk out at my harsh words, but instead she stands up straighter and shakes her head. "I don't believe you. I think you're lying to both of us." More tears are falling now, but she remains strong as she pulls her dress off over her head, followed by everything underneath. Her eyes never leave mine as she removes every last barrier between us and stands exposed in front of me. "If this is the only way you'll talk to me then here I am, Tristan. This is me, naked and ready to tell the truth for once. And the truth is I love you. I'm in love with you, Tristan, and I always will be. I don't know how to be me without you. And I know you love me, too. We're wrong for each other in all the right ways. I need you . . . and you need me, too."

Now I know without a doubt that I'm a stupid, selfish bastard, because it's not Hazel's well-being that keeps me from wrapping her in my arms and making all her hurt disappear. It's my own fear that while I might be able to take her pain away, mine would only twist deeper. *I don't know how to love you, Hazel, and I'm afraid I might lose myself again if I try.* That's the real truth.

I bend down and pick up Hazel's clothes. Her bravery and openness is about to shatter every bit of my resolve and I can't bear to face it. I really am a fucking coward.

"I don't need anybody, Hazel. You had your chance but you chose drugs instead, remember? We ended the second you made that choice." My voice is ragged and sharp as I shove her clothes back into her arms to cover the things I don't want to face anymore. I take my keys out of my pocket and drop them on top. "You can take my truck back. Keep it, for all I care. I don't want to see you anymore." *I can't see you anymore.*

I turn and leave and I don't look back. If I do, I'll see just how much my words destroy her.

I guess that's the thing about knowing someone so well— you know exactly how to hurt them in the worst way.

CHAPTER

thirty-one

Five Years Ago

Tristan

WHEN HAZEL MAKES HER CHOICE there's nothing left to say, so I simply leave. I wish I could say I made it all the way back to my car without looking back, but then I'd be an idiot and a liar.

Instead I decide to build a house.

Or start to, at least.

I spend every single day visiting the spot I bought, and I truly believe Hazel will come back to me. Will come back to us.

I do this for three months before realizing there is no fucking point. She's gone and she's never coming back. I wasn't enough to change her.

I wasn't enough, period.

So I smash my hammer through what was supposed to be our future kitchen wall and I pray on my fucking knees to any god that might listen to make me forget Hazel Blake ever existed.

CHAPTER

thirty-two

Tristan

LIKE SOME SORT OF CRUEL, sick joke, the day I end things with Hazel at the beach house is the same day I find out my mother died.

An overdose. Too much of a drug she knew she couldn't handle, but also couldn't live without.

You'd think saying goodbye to both of them would feel like a fresh start, but honestly I feel . . . unfinished.

These women may have burnt and broken me, but they also shaped me. Every action and every word has carved out a piece of the man that is Tristan Sharp. Without them, he wouldn't exist.

So how does he move on? How does he leave them behind?

"You ready?"

I look up from the spot on my living room carpet that I've been fixated on for hours. Or maybe it's only been minutes. Who the hell can tell anymore? Logan is standing there in a black suit that matches mine, looking sad, but not as lost. He's accepted our mom's faults a lot better than I have, but I know this is hard for him, too. I'm lucky to have him around to hold together the pieces I'm not ready to handle.

He really is the better brother. Don't tell him I said that.

I push myself off the couch and nod, even though I'm not sure how ready I am.

LOGAN PULLS HIS BLACK RANGE Rover into the church parking lot. We climb the big, stone steps leading up to the ornate wooden doors, but before we cross through I hesitate.

We used to go to church when we were little—one of the few things consistent between our mother's house and the various foster homes we lived in—but God and I haven't exactly been tight lately.

Don't get me wrong; I have faith. I think. I believe in *something*, I'm just not sure exactly what.

I used to pray my mom would get better. Then I would pray for Hazel to get better. When neither of them did, I prayed to forget them, and we all know how well that worked out. It's hard to believe you're much good in this world when your life has been filled with unanswered prayers. I'm not even worthy enough to listen to, in God's opinion.

I think about all the questions Hazel has asked me over the past few weeks. She listened like she actually heard me.

A bell tolling above snaps me from my reverie. Logan claps his hand on my shoulder and guides me over the threshold. In the lobby, he dips two fingers in the fountain of holy water and makes the sign of the cross on his forehead, chest, and shoulders. I do the same, out of respect, but I feel like a fraud.

As we walk down the center aisle I notice most of the pews are empty. Of the few people that are there, I recognize even fewer.

Logan and I choose an empty pew in the second row. It seems wrong to sit in the first.

The casket is already in front, draped in an ivory cloth with a giant cross stamped on top.

Her husband made all the arrangements. When he called to tell Logan and me the news he asked if we wanted a say in the service. We politely declined. It felt right that he took care of it. He knew her better than we did, anyway.

The priest stands at the podium, addressing everyone with a reading from the Bible. His voice vibrates through the quiet room, echoing loudly off the vaulted ceiling:

There is an appointed time for everything,
and a time for every affair under the heavens.
A time to give birth, and a time to die;
a time to plant, and a time to uproot the plant.
A time to kill, and a time to heal;
a time to tear down, and a time to build.
A time to weep, and a time to laugh;
a time to mourn, and a time to dance.
A time to scatter stones, and a time to gather them;
a time to embrace, and a time to be far from embraces.
A time to seek, and a time to lose;
a time to keep, and a time to cast away.
A time to rend, and a time to sew;
a time to be silent, and a time to speak.
A time to love, and a time to hate;
a time of war, and a time of peace.

The priest's poignant words dim as I try to focus on something, anything, other than death. I stare in front of me without really seeing. My mind, of course, wanders to Hazel, and a sense of calm folds over me. I still don't know how I feel about God or religion or faith, but something about being here makes me feel at peace—lets me know it's OK that I'm not sure what to think or how to feel.

I can't help but wonder what Hazel is doing right this very second. I picture all the times I've been with her. What did we say? What did we do? I think about how with us there always does seem to be a time for everything.

Sometimes we joke and sometimes we're serious.

Sometimes we talk and sometimes we don't.

Sometimes we hurt and sometimes we heal.

And sometimes we fuck.

Oh, how we fuck.

I shake my head and wonder if there's something majorly fucked up about me that I'm sitting here thinking about screwing Hazel while I'm in a church at my mother's funeral. I should be thinking about my mom. I should be thinking about our childhood and our past and all the time I spent with her.

Except that would only be to honor her, not because I want to. Rather than dwell on the past, I want to picture a future with Hazel.

A future where sometimes we joke and sometimes we're serious.

A future where sometimes we talk and sometimes we don't.

A future where sometimes we fuck, but sometimes we make love.

A future where sometimes we might hurt, but we *always* heal. Together.

It sounds like a fucking perfect life, but it's not real. And having to live with that harsh reality is my penance, my punishment, for stupidly letting her back into my life.

If there is a God, he's one sick bastard.

I bow my head as the priest finishes up the reading. A few lines in particular weigh on my mind for the rest of the service.

"What now is

has already been;
what is to be,
already is"

It sounds important, but what in the flying fuck does it mean?

I LEAVE MY MOTHER'S FUNERAL feeling more unsettled than ever. Logan and I end up at Chaser's, sitting at the bar with two beers, although neither of us has taken a sip.

"*Fuuuuck,*" I groan, spinning around on the stool so my back is to the bar.

Logan has his index finger on the top of his bottle, tracing the rounded opening. "I hear ya, brother," is all he says, knowing it's the only way I'm capable of communicating right now.

I close my eyes and take slow, deep breaths, something I've seen Hazel do countless times. After a few seconds I do feel a little calmer so I open my eyes and look at Logan.

"Have you forgiven her?" I ask.

"Our mother?" He shrugs. "I don't really think there is anything to forgive her for."

I scoff. "How about for abandoning us? For making us feel like we weren't enough to make her stop doing stupid shit?"

He shifts sideways to face me. "I didn't feel that way. You felt that way?"

I just stare at him. I don't admit the truth, but I don't deny it either.

He shakes his head. "Yes, her choices were pretty shitty, I'll give you that. But I would rather have lived in ten halfway decent homes than one really shitty one. She was in no position to raise us, and who knows where we would have ended up if she had tried?"

"I've wondered the exact same fucking thing," I mutter bitterly. Maybe my brother's life is all peaches and cream, but from where I'm sitting, a different life wouldn't have been so bad. At least then I would never have met Hazel Blake.

As soon as the thought crosses my mind, I instantly hate myself, because I know deep down I would hate a life where Hazel Blake never existed even more than this tortured agony.

As if reading my fucking mind by some miracle of twin telepathy, Logan states matter-of-factly, "You do know they're different, right?"

I look away, pretending not to know exactly what he means. "What the fuck are you talking about?"

"You're really not ready to admit it, are you? Shit, T. I'll give you points for consistency." He drops his chin to his chest and chuckles silently before looking back at me. "Stop being the biggest fucking idiot in the entire world, OK? Hazel Blake is not like our mother. She got clean and she chose you and your head is so far up your ass only stupid shit comes out of your mouth."

I stare at my brother. Fuck it if he isn't right, but I'm still not ready to accept it. If I do, that means I have to face a whole lot of feelings I'm not used to.

Dammit, I hate it when he's right. I hate that I have to deal with this. I hate myself and I hate this bar and I want to hate Hazel, but I *especially* hate how I haven't actually hated her in a very long time.

"*Fuuuuck,*" I groan again, still unable to put any of my thoughts into words.

"Yup," is all Logan says in response.

Feeling antsy, I hop off the stool. "I need some air," I grunt, heading for the side door.

I shove it open and clasp my hands behind my head. I pace around the alley, trying to get a handle on things. I haven't felt this jacked up since the last time I found myself in this very spot, trying—and failing—to fuck the feeling away.

As if on cue, the door swings open again and Tiffany appears.

I look up at the sky. *God, if you're up there, you really are sick. Funny, but sick.*

I can't help but chuckle to myself. It's either that or cry, and we all know that's not going to happen.

When I look up at Tiffany I notice a strange look in her eyes, but as soon as she sees me she plasters on a smile.

"Fancy meeting you here." She stalks closer, running her fingers down my arm.

I study her face, and while she outwardly appears to be the same old Tiffany I've always known, something is definitely different. Her voice, actions, and clothing hint at nothing but a good time, but her eyes look . . . sad? Has she always looked like this? Have I never noticed it before?

I gently grab her wrist, stopping her from reaching my belt.

"Really? That's the second time you've turned me down, Tristan. I promise there won't be a third." Her voice is confident and sassy, but when I see the hurt that flashes in her eyes, I finally recognize the look. *Rejection.*

In this one look I can tell she has just as many insecurities as I do. We're the exact same type of person. We fear being rejected, so we offer only a small, superficial piece of ourselves. It's not about having power over each other, it's about helping each other to feel connected to something, even if only on a physical level. Sex is easy—it's primal and carnal and you don't have to think about it. It's obvious and tangible and it allows us to hide our deeper feelings behind a shield of raw pleasure.

But it doesn't connect us in a way that truly matters.

I take a step back, sincerely admitting, "I'm sorry, Tiffany.

We can't give each other what we really need."

She crosses her arms, but her eyes soften. I think she understands exactly what I'm saying. I give her shoulder a light squeeze before stepping around her to head back inside.

I turn down sex with Tiffany because I don't think I want to bury my feelings anymore.

And that, my friend, scares the ever-living shit out of me.

STEP NINE: TRUTH

We made direct amends to such people wherever possible, except when to do so would injure them or others.

CHAPTER

thirty-three

Hazel

"HOW'S MY LITTLE NEPHEW DOING?" I look down at the cutest kid I've ever seen, cradled in Kelley's arms.

"He's great. His mom? Not so much. I've barely slept in weeks." Kelley tries to laugh, but it ends on a yawn.

I reach my arms out and she places Caden on my lap.

I was actually surprised that Kelley asked me to meet her for coffee. We've become a little closer over the past few weeks, as I got into the habit of texting to ask if there was anything I could do to help with Caden, but I figured since my blowout with Ryan she would be taking his side.

"Thanks for meeting me. I really needed to get out and figured Caden could use a little Auntie time." Kelley takes a sip of her coffee. She closes her eyes and looks like she's having quite the orgasmic moment as she swallows it down.

I giggle and let Caden grab my finger. "Anytime. I'm just glad you're not mad at me, too."

"Why would I be mad at you?"

"I just figured since Ry and I had it out at the party over

Tristan you'd be upset with me, too."

She shrugs. "Just because I love your brother doesn't mean I have to agree with him. I know he acts that way because he cares about you, but I also think it's hard for him to see that you're an adult now, too. You're entitled to be with whomever you want."

I smile, really glad my brother was smart enough to hang onto this girl.

"But you might want to cut him a little slack. He really does want what's best for you."

"Yeah, he really thought about that when he left home as fast as he could, leaving me behind," I can't help but blurt bitterly.

Kelley frowns. "I don't think Ryan left you, he just needed to get away from your mother."

"I get it . . . it's not surprising. First my dad left, then Ryan, and now . . ." I trail off, deciding I'd rather not think about Tristan walking out on me. "Well, now my mom is all I have left, and we all know that's not saying much."

Kelley looks concerned before gently asking, "I know it's not my place, but why do you stay with her?"

I sigh. "I know she's not the easiest person to get along with, but I owe her my life for forcing me into rehab. She can't be all bad if she cared enough about me to do that, right?"

Kelley looks like she wants to say something, but stops herself at the last second.

"What?" I ask, getting a weird feeling that she knows something I don't.

She looks unsure before admitting, "I shouldn't tell you this since Ryan would kill me, but screw it—I birthed his spawn so he owes me. Hazel, your mother isn't the one responsible for sending you to rehab. Ryan is. I guess he felt like he couldn't reach you so he threatened to air all your family's dirty laundry if she didn't get you help."

I take a second to try and process this information. If what Kelley is saying is true, then everything I thought about my mother—and my brother—has changed.

"What? Why wouldn't he tell me?" Caden decides that now is a good time to squirm around in my lap like an inchworm.

Kelley shrugs. "Because he holds himself responsible for you getting into trouble in the first place. He hasn't given me all the details, but I can tell he carries around a lot of guilt about whatever happened. Now he's just happy you are doing so well. He didn't want anything to jeopardize that."

I shake my head, wondering if my life could get any more screwed up. "He gave me such a hard time about Tristan I thought he was just being an overbearing big brother. I didn't realize he had his own guilt to deal with." I hand the squirming baby back to his mom.

"How are things going with you and Tristan, anyway?" Kelley asks, settling Caden in his stroller.

Speaking of complicated . . .

I look down at my lap, feeling embarrassed by everything that happened.

Picking up on my hesitation, Kelley calls me out. "It went to shit, didn't it?"

I chuckle, even though I don't find it remotely funny. "Completely."

"What happened? Was it about what happened at the park?"

I play with the plastic lid on my paper cup. "Yes. No. Maybe?" I groan. "Ugh. I don't know. I was ready to go all in but he wasn't. The End."

"He wasn't ready, or he wasn't willing?" Kelley takes another sip of her coffee.

"Does it matter? Same difference."

"No, there's a huge difference. If he isn't ready that means he's just being stubborn and there's still time for a happily ever after. If he isn't willing . . . well then, that means it's time to start a new story."

Kelley smiles. Her romantic optimism is almost contagious.

Almost. "We've had some bad fights, Kelley, but this was the worst. I'm not sure we can come back from it." Maybe it wasn't exactly a *fight* per se, but close enough. It's the easiest way to describe it, since fights are often full of hurtful words and harsh realizations, which is essentially what happened.

"Just remember, a fight isn't over until the make-up sex begins," Kelley replies with a wink.

I genuinely laugh for the first time in weeks.

SPENDING THE AFTERNOON WITH KELLEY not only helped me feel the tiniest bit better, but it also made me realize just how many people I hurt with my addiction. I knew I hurt Tristan, but Ryan? I never realized how much my actions affected him, too.

Which is why I'm knocking on his apartment door three days later, hoping he'll still speak to me. I'll take it as a good sign that Darrin, the security guy who guards the front lobby of my brother's fancy apartment complex, didn't tackle me to prevent me from going upstairs.

I hit the button for the fifth floor and knock lightly when I get to apartment E4. When Ryan opens the door I smile shyly and wave a white tissue from my pocket in the air.

"You're lucky you're my favorite sister, you know that?" he says on a laugh before letting me inside.

"Then it's a good thing I'm your only sister, too, huh?" I grin.

We head to the living room and sit quietly on the large black leather couch. I'm not sure why I feel so nervous, so I look around the apartment to distract myself. I've only been here once before and I'm happy to see what a great life my brother has made for himself and now his little family. The dark wood and clean-lined furniture that make the place so striking are now nicely complimented by a few framed pictures, some throw pillows, and of course a bunch of baby toys.

"Kelley took Caden out for the afternoon. I think she mentioned going to see Kinsley so I'm sure she'll be gone a while." Ryan must sense my anxiousness.

I take a deep breath. "I wanted to come by to apologize . . . for everything."

"I guess I should be saying the same thing."

"Well you were kind of an ass to Tristan . . ." We both chuckle. "But I want you to know that what I went through wasn't your fault, either."

Ryan shakes his head in protest. "I should have been there for you. I should have tried to help more. I saw you were hurting, but I was too busy fucking up my own life to do anything about it. But that's no excuse. I'm your brother and it was my job to protect you."

"You did all you could have done, Ry. I wasn't going to listen to anyone, let alone my annoying big brother." I playfully punch him in the arm to lighten the mood. Our family has never really been one for deep conversations, but it feels good to have a real talk with Ryan for once. "Kelley told me how it was you who wanted me to get help."

I can see Ryan's jaw tense.

"Please don't be mad at her. I wish you had told me years ago, but I get why you didn't. I felt so alone and I thought I was just ruining my own life with my choices. I couldn't see how much they affected everyone around me. It was selfish, though, and I'm sorry I ever made you think it was your fault. I promise it wasn't. It was my own self-destructive nature."

"We seem to have that in common." He shakes his head sorrowfully.

"But you got past it, and look at you now. You're successful, have a beautiful family, loyal friends . . . I have to admit I'm kind of jealous."

"You can have all that, too, Hazel."

I shake my head. "I don't think I'm able to escape the Blake DNA. I seem to have more in common with our father, messing up lives and leaving nothing but heartbreak in my wake."

Ryan pauses. "I went to see him, you know . . . dear old dad. Shortly before Caden was born."

My eyes go wide. "Why the hell would you do that?"

"Because I wanted to punch him in the fucking face." Ryan snickers, then continues. "I thought the same thing you're thinking, that I was too much like him. Kelley and I went through a rough time and I wanted to confront him. But what I saw was a guy who gave up, and I knew that wasn't going to be me. So I made the choice to fight for what I have. That's all it takes to break free, Hazel. You just have to want it bad enough."

I contemplate my brother's words, wondering when he got so mature. I think fatherhood suits him, and suddenly I feel very proud to be his sister, which is the first time in my life I've ever been proud of being a Blake.

But when I think about how I tried to fight for Tristan, yet he still wanted nothing to do with me, I feel sick. "And what if that's not enough? What if *I'm* not enough?"

"As much as it kills me to say this, I think Tristan loves you. After you told me what he did for you that night I started to re-think all of our interactions involving you."

Ryan runs his hands through his hair, looking reminiscent.

"Deep down I knew Tristan would never hurt you. He might

be an immature asshole, but he's still one of the good ones." He shakes his head. "It was easier to blame him than you, though. Hell, it was easier to blame him than myself. I admit that at first I was fucking pissed that you guys kept the truth from me for all these years, but once I calmed down I realized I wouldn't have wanted to hear it anyway. I think I always knew he had nothing to do with your addiction, but he let me give him shit for years to protect you. A guy only does that for one reason."

I lift my eyes, feeling a sudden surge of hope, before the memory of Tristan's distant, hollow eyes clouds my vision. "Maybe he used to love me, but I don't think he does anymore. I hurt him when he didn't deserve one bit of it. I can't blame him for hating me."

"Can I give you one piece of brotherly advice?"

I shrug and nod at the same time.

"Guys are stupid, Hazel. Really fucking stupid sometimes. We let our pride get in the way and we don't like to admit our flaws. I've known Tristan a long time and the dude has an ego the size of Texas. He'd never want to admit defeat, especially if he's been burned before. But if he let me bust his balls for your sake, then I'd say he just needs a little more time to figure his shit out. You need to be willing to do the same."

"Mom says a flaw is a weakness and people bring it upon themselves. She doesn't think people can change. Maybe she's right, because I still seem to be causing all sorts of pain for the people I care about."

Ryan is quiet for a minute before looking me in the eye. "Does Tristan make you happy?" His voice is pained, as if he's having an internal struggle about whether or not he really wants to know the answer.

I nod.

"Then fuck what anybody else thinks. Especially Mom. Do

you really think she knows how life works? A lot of times things need to get worse before they get better, but we have to fix our mistakes on our own in order to change. Admitting our faults is a sign of strength. That's how we grow. You can't just give up, Hazel. Not if it's your chance to be happy."

I know without a doubt that Tristan makes me the happiest I've ever been, but I would sacrifice every bit of my own happiness if it means he can have his. "I don't think I deserve him, Ryan. At least not yet. He once told me that in order to help someone, you have to make it about them and not you. I can't be with him just to make myself happy. That's not fair to either of us. I need to fix my own life before I can build one with him. We can't make it if we're stuck in the past."

Ryan reaches out and squeezes my hand. "Then it sounds like you need to figure out a way to move forward."

I smile and squeeze his hand back. "I think I know exactly where to start."

CHAPTER

thirty-four

Hazel

"WELL, WHADDYA THINK?" I CLAP my hands together, not even trying to hide my excitement.

My mom walks around the car, taking in its rusted paint, cracked side mirror, and dented bumper. "Honestly, Hazel, this looks like a death trap. I wouldn't pay for this with Monopoly money, let alone real American dollars."

I smile wider. I honestly don't care if she likes it or not. This car is a symbol of my newfound independence, and I bought it all on my own.

Once I found out my mom wasn't quite as selfless as I thought she was by getting me into rehab, I realized I could let all my conflicted feelings about our relationship go. I'm ready to forget the past and work solely on building a future. If she wants to be a part of that I'll give her the chance, but it won't be because I'm indebted to her.

She takes in my beaming face and crosses her arms. "At least park it around the back. I don't want our neighbors to see it in the driveway."

With that she turns on her heel and stalks back inside.

I giggle to myself and hop in the driver's seat, petting the dashboard as I take it all in.

The door handle may be broken and a few of the radio knobs might be missing, but I've never loved an inanimate object so much in my life. To know I worked, saved, and earned this without having to rely on anyone else makes me feel like I can do anything.

And I've got to say, it's even better than being high.

I reach for my phone, but after sliding my finger across the screen I stop, my enthusiasm turning to sadness.

There is only one friend I really want to tell about this, but he's no longer mine.

I rest my head back on the seat and close my eyes. I think a small part of me hoped that by buying this car I wouldn't feel like I needed Tristan so much. I've been dependent all my life, needing my mom for money, drugs for escape, and Tristan for . . . well, to breathe. To make me feel whole.

But that wasn't fair, expecting him to fix me. Countless times he tried to help me, and couldn't. I'm to blame for ever letting him think everything that he did wasn't good enough. That *he* wasn't good enough.

Feeling restless, I start up the car and drive away from the house. I drive for hours, finally ending up on the road to Mr. Turner's beach house. I park outside it and grab my earbuds, then almost immediately shove them back in my bag.

If there were ever a perfect time or place to confront my thoughts and feelings, this would be it.

I walk down the path and sink into the sand. I've spent the past couple of weeks trying to piece together the broken parts of what Tristan and I used to be, but I've come to realize I had it all wrong.

Tristan and I could never go back to who we were.

We weren't supposed to.

As I watch the place where the surf meets the sand, I realize Tristan Sharp is a wave. One that comes crashing in, wild and impulsive, yet strong and measured, bringing you along for the ride until it breaks on the shore, at which point you either have to let it go by, standing strong as it recedes without you, or risk getting sucked into the unpredictable rip current that can drag you under.

By definition, waves are classified based on three factors: 1. The disturbing force that creates them; 2. The extent to which the disturbing force continues to influence them after formation; and 3. The extent to which the restoring force weakens them.

1. I am the disturbing force that created the monster wave that is now Tristan Sharp.

2. I should have stayed away, but instead I was reckless and stubborn and tested the laws of nature by returning to him.

3. I selfishly thought our physical relationship could some-how defy gravity and weaken all of the hurt and pain that has built up over the last five years, but instead it all got sucked back into our dangerous pull, generating a truth explosion that caused the tsunami that just wiped out our entire relationship.

Yes, Tristan Sharp is a wave that turned into a storm.

And the sad part is that I would still gladly drown in every single bit of him.

I once heard that you know you truly love someone when you don't hate them for breaking your heart. If that's the case, there is no doubt about my feelings for Tristan, because I don't hate him. Not even a little bit. I never did. I actually understand perfectly why he had to walk away, and I know it's all my fault. I broke us five years ago when I chose feeling nothing over feeling everything.

And that's the ugly truth I have to live with.

I've beaten myself up countless times trying to figure out why I chose to hurt him, of all people, but the best I can come up with is that it was my fucked-up way of trying to save him. I wasn't in my right mind, but I can only hope that deep down I knew I was drowning and I needed to sever our tie before I took him down with me. Either way, it will always be my biggest regret.

Now I need to move beyond it. Despite my reservations, I really have changed. It's time to start a new chapter.

I reach into my bag and pull out the Red Cross CNA application I've been carrying around for weeks.

Tristan may not be in my life anymore, but he will always be a part of me and I want to make him proud. He believed in me even when I didn't deserve it, and I want to show him it wasn't wasted effort.

I pull out a pen and start filling in my name, age, sex, and address.

This is for both of us.

When I'm finished filling out the form I start up my new car and head to the post office to mail it. After that I just drive, learning how to navigate my newfound freedom.

STEP TEN: LOYALTY

We continued to take personal inventory and when we were wrong promptly admitted it.

CHAPTER

thirty-five

Tristan

"LET'S DO SOMETHING TONIGHT."

"No thanks."

"How about Chaser's?"

"No."

"Dirty D's across town? I hear they have a new dancer who does this trick with a lollipop and a cigar."

"Fuck no. Hand me that board."

"Man, you're no fun anymore." Logan pouts and hands me the piece of plywood I nodded to. "Why the hell are you so interested in finishing this place all of a sudden, anyway? You've had a half-finished house for years and seemed perfectly fine with it, and now it's like you're Bob the fucking Builder . . . on crack or something."

I shrug, not sure where to even begin to explain things. Based on our conversation at the bar after our mom's funeral, I know Logan knows way more than he often lets on, but he has the decency to pretend like that conversation never happened. He understands I need time to process.

It's been four weeks since I abandoned a naked and broken Hazel Blake. I really thought it was the only way to stop our cycle of hurt, but the pain has only deepened.

For the second time in my life I tried to forget her and for the second time in my life I failed.

A few days after the funeral I came out of my apartment to find my truck, the keys sitting on the front seat in an envelope. Inside the envelope was also a picture of me asleep on Hazel's bedroom floor, looking completely contented, satisfied, and happy.

A picture of me through Hazel's eyes.

Scrawled across the photo in black marker, right across my chest, were the words *Hazel was here.*

Yup, she was there—written on me, wrapped around me, buried under my skin and permanently etched into my heart. She was and still is. Always has been, always will be.

But I spent so much time blaming her, hating her for the past, that I didn't even try to see how much she's changed. I was so busy trying to prove that *I* was different, that *I* didn't need her, I couldn't even see it was me who broke us this time. And it's something I don't know how to fix.

The first time I let her walk away. The second time I didn't want to give her the chance to leave, so I left first. But man, I've come to realize I'd rather take the pain of loving Hazel Blake over the pain of losing her any damn day.

"Seriously, I haven't seen you in weeks and when you asked for help nailing things, I thought it was code for something involving women. Not, well, actual nails." Logan looks disappointed as I hammer the board into place.

"I knew it was the only way to get you out here." I try to keep things light, even though heaviness grips my entire being.

Before Logan can form a comeback we hear a truck pull up

the dirt path.

Ryan gets out and walks toward us with his hands in his pockets, stopping right at the wood-framed doorway.

Logan says, "Ry, please tell my brother he's being a pussy and needs to get out more. First you and Lucas wife up, and now this guy would rather work all damn day and night than go out and get laid. I need to get some new friends."

Ryan attempts a half-hearted smirk, but remains quiet. I also don't move, not sure what in the hell to say.

Logan looks between us, picking up on the obvious vibe shift. "Manual labor really isn't my thing, so I'm gonna get going. You ladies have fun." He retreats to his own car, leaving Ryan and I to stare each other down.

Finally Ryan speaks. "You should have fucking told me."

I sigh. "It wasn't my place."

His eyes narrow on me, serious and a little bit threatening. "You love her?"

I meet the intensity of his stare, not backing down. I nod.

"Well then you better figure your shit out."

Ryan then picks up the next piece of board and helps me maneuver it into place beside the one I just secured. We work together for the next hour without saying another word. We don't need to.

AFTER RYAN LEAVES AND I start to pack it in myself, I hear another vehicle pull up the drive. Mr. Turner gets out and whistles admiringly as he walks up to where I'm putting some tools back in their box.

"You sure have made a lot of progress on this place. Looking good, son, looking good."

I grunt in response.

"Well, I just wanted to come by and let you know that I've been doing some painting up at the beach house. Virginia decided it was time for a change."

The mere mention of the beach house has my jaw tensing and my skin tingling.

"Strangest thing, though. There's this girl that's been coming up and sitting out there on the beach. A pretty little thing . . . just comes and sits for hours in the same spot. You wouldn't happen to know anything about that, would you?"

I know this is his way of telling me what to do without telling me what to do, and knowing he's talking about Hazel has my heart beating faster. I still have no words, but the way Mr. Turner laughs and heads back to his truck tells me he isn't expecting any.

"Fixing this house isn't going to fix things with your girl, so get your head out of your ass and tell her you love her, will ya? That way we can all finally see you happy," he calls before driving off.

As I watch the cloud of dust behind his truck settle I know he's right.

Hazel was willing to admit her past mistakes and put her heart on the line, so maybe it's about fucking time I do the same.

STEP ELEVEN: ABSOLUTION

We sought through prayer and meditation to improve our conscious contact with God as we understood Him, praying only for knowledge of His will for us and the power to carry that out.

CHAPTER
thirty-six

Tristan

I PULL MY CAR OVER and cut the ignition. I say a silent prayer that she'll be here.

The sky is overcast and it looks like rain as I walk down the sandy path to the stretch of beach behind Mr. Turner's property. As I pass the house I stop, remembering everything that happened the last time I was here.

But for the first time, the pain of the past doesn't make me want to put up all my defenses. I accept everything that's happened for what it's taught me, but the only thing I can focus on is my future. And that's a feeling I sure as shit could get used to.

I continue down the back path and my prayers are finally answered. As soon as the sand comes into view I see her: the girl I'm no longer afraid to love.

OK, that's a lie. I'm fucking terrified.

But for the first time, I'm OK with that.

Things might still turn to shit in the end, but it won't be because I'm too scared to try. I truly believe Hazel has changed, and what I want more than anything is to be her second chance.

Hey, being a pessimistic bastard hasn't worked out for me too well, so I figure it's time to try the whole optimism thing.

She's sitting on the beach, staring out into the water as the wind whips her hair around her face, looking like a beacon of fiery light amidst the gray. I take a minute to look at her.

God, she's so fucking beautiful.

I walk up and sink down beside her. She doesn't look at me, but by the way her body tenses she knows it's me. We sit in silence for a while, both lost in the sound of the waves crashing against the shore. Every time the water hits the sand I can feel the slightest mist spray across my face. It feels like a new beginning.

I position myself to face Hazel and for the first time in months I get to see her. *Really* see her. I cradle her cheek in my hand, leaning forward to press my lips to hers. I can taste salt on her skin and I feel her gasp as we connect, each of us swallowing the other's pain and breathing life back into our souls.

I reluctantly pull back to tug a familiar black box out of my pocket. I hold it in my hands, twisting it around in my fingers. I'm sure as fuck ready to rewrite the past.

Still staring down at the box, I muse, "There was a time I thought I wasn't good enough for you. That I wasn't good enough, period. I've come to realize it was true, but only because I was too much of a stubborn asshole to prove myself wrong." I look up at Hazel. "But I refuse to let that be my truth anymore. I'm so fucking right for you, just like you are for me. That's *our* truth. I'm in love with you, Hazel Blake, and I want to spend the rest of my life loving you." I extend the box toward her. "We have another chance to choose the way we want our lives to go right now."

This time there is only one choice, and I know without a shadow of a doubt that I'm all in. I am so fucking in.

Hazel slowly reaches out for the box, but stops.

My heart beats faster.

She looks up to me with tears in her eyes and moves her hand to my chest, placing it right over my heart. "I choose *you*, Tristan. From now on and forever and always, it will always be you."

Her words heal every broken part of me and I kiss her again, fully and deeply. I move my hand over hers and wrap the black box between our fingers, urging her to open it.

She pulls the top back to reveal a key. I push myself to standing and pull her up behind me. She looks surprised and confused, but I just smile mischievously and say, "I want to take you somewhere."

CHAPTER

thirty-seven

Hazel

WHEN TRISTAN DRIVES DOWN THE familiar dirt driveway I feel butterflies in my stomach. As we approach the lot, I'm surprised to see that the house, while still not completely finished, looks like it's been worked on quite a bit.

We walk up to what I imagine is supposed to be the front. The walls aren't up yet, but a purple door is framed in the middle of the open sides. I find myself speechless as I walk up to it in what feels like slow motion.

Tristan smiles and nods to the key in my hand before pointing to the doorknob. "Why don't you give it a try?"

I laugh. "You know I can just walk around it, right? I don't think a lock is doing you any good right now," I can't help but tease.

Tristan gets a serious look and stalks across the porch toward me. He grabs my hips and kisses me in such an unexpectedly gentle way that I'm left breathless as he pulls back and whispers in my ear, "Just put your key in my damn lock, will ya?"

I do exactly as he says, and when I twist the key I hear a

small *click* as the door pops open. I step inside and right in the middle of the unfinished room is a blanket with pillows spread on the floor, along with a bottle of sparkling cider sitting in an ice bucket. When I look up, directly above it is a simple, delicate ring hanging from the rafters by a piece of string.

My right hand flies to my mouth as Tristan unties it and slips it onto my left ring finger.

"Hazel Blake, will you marry me?"

I nod repeatedly, whispering, "*Yes*," over and over as I throw myself into his arms. My mouth finds his and we stumble to the ground.

I lie on top of him and we both pause at the same time. Suddenly there doesn't seem to be any hurry. In the past, it always felt like we were racing some invisible clock—a clock that kept time with the past—and we were just waiting for it to catch up with us. But now? Now it feels like we have all the time in the world.

I sit up and pull my shirt over my head before shimmying out of my jeans. I run my fingers under the hem of Tristan's shirt, feeling the strength of his toned stomach. I slide my hands slowly up his chest, feeling his heartbeat race beneath my palm. I love that we make each other come to life.

I pull his shirt from his body and as I begin to unbutton his jeans he reaches into his pocket. I stop him. "I want us to feel all of each other, with nothing in the way of that."

His eyes turn dark and hungry and he pulls me closer to him. He sits up so I'm straddling him and his mouth finds my nipple. I arch back with a moan, unable to contain the pure ecstasy surging through my body. I dig my fingers into his shoulders as I feel him fill me.

This time, as we make love, it's not about hurting or punishing and it's not about winning or losing. It's not even about reaching that ultimate peak.

It's about feeling each other in this moment. No expectations. No rules. No end.

And nothing so unanchored has ever felt this sure.

As Tristan's teeth scrape over my skin he vows, "This is home, Hazel. This is our home and it's the place we're going to spend the rest of our lives together."

We continue to move together in perfect rhythm until our bodies meld into one being. We fearlessly come apart together, never letting go.

Day turns into night and for the first time I find myself looking forward to what comes next. We lie back and watch the stars through the open, unfinished roof.

This is home.

And it's perfect.

STEP TWELVE: FOREVER

Having had a spiritual awakening as a result of these steps, we tried to carry this message to addicts, and to practice these principles in all our affairs.

Tristan

"REALLY, T? YOU BUILT HER a fucking house? I thought all that *Notebook* style shit was only in movies. Way to make the rest of us look like losers."

"I bet Kinsley is regretting choosing you over me now."

I grin at Lucas as he walks back to his wife, knowing he's only giving me shit because he's happy for me.

I insisted on throwing Hazel a party to celebrate her getting both her CNA certification *and* her first job offer. Since I just finished up our house last week, it seemed like the perfect time to have everyone over. I'm so fucking proud of her. She'll never know how much, even though I tell her all the time.

I also show her, thoroughly and repeatedly. Sometimes we even take pictures of it.

And no, you can't see them. Fucking pervert.

From the front porch I look out across the yard and see all the people I care about in one place.

Lucas, Kinsley, and my brother are off making gaga faces at Caden while Ryan and Kelley try to steal kisses when they think no one is looking. I even saw the sly bastard grab her ass three separate times. One night when we were all out at dinner we agreed there should be no more secrets, so they finally admitted the real story behind their relationship. I, of course, will give Ryan endless amounts of shit about it, but it was a relief to know that Hazel and I aren't the only effed-up ones when it comes to love.

Speaking of Hazel, she's in the driveway showing off her piece-of-shit car to the Turners as her mother looks on with an embarrassed scowl. I was surprised Hazel wanted to invite her mom, but I wasn't about to get in the middle of that. When Holly arrived she took one look at the purple door and said, "Well it certainly is . . . *colorful.*" Hazel smiled at me and whispered that it was as close to a compliment as we were going to get.

And for the first time ever I found out I actually agree with Holly Blake on one thing—the crap-mobile looks like a death trap. But I also know how much it means to Hazel, so I keep my mouth shut. Sometimes she'll take me for a drive on the weekends, after we finish our volunteer shift at the Greenside Rehab Center. Hazel said she wanted to give back, and I decided it might do me some good, too. I figure I've done enough bad shit in my life that the good karma can't hurt. And I admit it feels right to help heal other people together, after all the hurt we've caused.

I stalk over to Hazel and throw my arm around her shoulders. She beams at me and I smile back.

For the first time my shit-eating grin is one hundred percent genuine—I am without a doubt the luckiest bastard alive.

The End.

Find out more

Want a little behind the scenes peek about the making of this book? Head on over to *https://jshbooks.com/books/sick-pleasure/behind-the-book/* for more!

acknowledgements

I'M GOING TO KEEP THESE short and sweet . . .

To the greatest husband ever—Clifford, I am forever thankful you're you.

To my family—You guys make me proud to be me.

To Heidi Fiedler—I can't thank you enough for recommending Pat to me! Match made in editorial heaven. <3

To Pat Dobie—I am so happy Heidi led me to you! Your incredible insight and enthusiasm over this book made writing this story exciting again. (Seriously, I was having quite the tough time before I sent you the first draft!) I loved this story and these characters from the beginning, but getting it to translate on the page was hard. You provided all the right notes in all the right places and I found myself eagerly checking my inbox just to hear what you were thinking. :)

To Kari March—Thank you again for an amazing cover.

To Christine and Nichole at Perfectly Publishable—Once again you two are the best for finalizing all the last minute details and making this book beautiful for all to read.

And finally, to anybody who reads this—You rock. End of story.

about the author

WHEN SHE'S NOT MAKING CONFETTI as head honcho over at The Confetti Bar (*theconfettibar.com*), co-dreaming with creative women through Monarch Workshop (*monarchworkshop.com*), and blogging about her health & wellness journey going sugar-free at Simple Unsweet (*simpleunsweet.com*), Jessica loves to spend her nights getting caught up in imaginary worlds.

She lives in central CT with her husband, Clifford, and the cutest cat EVER, named Curious.

She loves colorful things, making people smile, things that smell good, and is obsessed with lemon water. And glitter. Lots of glitter.

She also loves, well . . . love. (She's a sucker for a sweet story.)

You can check out what she's up to at *jshbooks.com* and on Instagram (@jshbooks)

Want to know anything else? Feel free to say hi at *lovejshbooks@gmail.com!*